THE **ALIEN** WHO CAME TO **DINNER**

THE **ALIEN** WHO **CAME** TO **DINNER**

BRUCE COVILLE

ILLUSTRATED BY
PAUL DAVIES

Hodder
Children's
Books

a division of Hodder Headline Limited

For Marie Lang, keeper of the keys,
Oddly Enough.

Text copyright © 2000 Bruce Coville
Illustrations copyright © 2000 Paul Davies

First published in the USA in 2000
as *Sixth Grade Alien 9: There's an Alien in My Backpack*
by Pocket Books, a division of Simon & Schuster Inc.

First published in Great Britain in 2000
by Hodder Children's Books

The right of Bruce Coville to be identified as the Author of
the Work has been asserted by him in accordance with
the Copyright, Designs and Patents Act 1988.

1 3 5 7 9 10 8 6 4 2

A Catalogue record for this book is available from
the British Library

ISBN 0 340 73642 9

Typeset by Avon Dataset Ltd, Bidford-on-Avon, Warks
Printed and bound in Great Britain by
Clays Ltd, St Ives plc, Bungay, Suffolk

Hodder Children's Books
a division of Hodder Headline Ltd
338 Euston Road
London NW1 3BH

CONTENTS

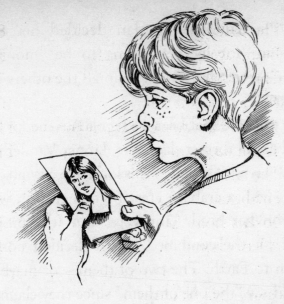

1

MISSING LINNSY

"Hey, monster maker," said Jordan Lynch as he sauntered into our classroom. "Why don't you go back to space where you belong?"

I sighed and slid down in my chair, trying to disappear. Jordan has always had a large collection of names he likes to call me – things like "boogerbreath", "dootbrain", and "buttface". But after Pleskit and I returned from our adventures on Billa Kindikan, Jordan decided his new nickname for me was going to be "monster maker", which hurt worse than all the others put together.

He calls me that because he blames me for the fact that our former classmate, Linnsy Vanderhof, is now a *veccir* – that is, she is locked in a symbiotic union with a crablike creature named Bur, who lives on her head. Linnsy *vec* Bur (the proper name for the combined being) decided not to return to Earth. The two of them – or maybe I should say "the one of them" since they claim to be a single entity are off somewhere exploring the galaxy, or doing business deals, or who knows what.

Anyway, it's hard enough to return to everyday life when you've just saved the entire civilized galaxy from collapse into chaos. If you happen to have lost one of your classmates in the process, it's infinitely worse – especially if she was one of the more popular kids in the class.

It doesn't help the churning that starts in my guts whenever Jordan calls me "monster maker" that sometimes I *do* blame myself for what happened to Linnsy. I know this is stupid. It was Maktel who got us trapped in Ellico *vec* Bur's spaceship. And it was Linnsy's own choice not to come back.

Well, Linnsy *vec* Bur's choice.

Half of me is worried sick about her. The other half is crazy jealous because *she's* doing what *I* had always dreamed of – exploring the galaxy.

I think about that at night, when I'm trying to get to sleep, which hasn't been so easy lately. It's one thing to dream about leaving home for the stars and another to actually do it. Until Linnsy made her choice I had never really thought about how my going would affect my mother. Now I have a better idea, partly because I go to talk to Linnsy's mom and dad a couple of times a week.

The Vanderhofs live in the apartment directly above ours. Fortunately, *they* don't seem to blame me for what happened – at least, not entirely. It helps that the Interplanetary Trading Federation brought them to Trader's Court, so they had a chance to see Linnsy before she took off with Bur.

Still, it's hard for them.

3

I think that's why Mrs Vanderhof keeps inviting me up for cookies and milk.

"We all have to let go of our children sooner or later," she'll say, dabbing at her eyes with a tissue. "I just wasn't r-r-r-ready t-t-to . . . oh, Mr Timothy!"

That's as far as she ever gets before she breaks down crying.

I'll confess that sometimes I cry, too. I miss Linnsy more than I could have imagined. Even though she had dropped me as a best friend when she sprinted ahead of me in the social decathlon (which hadn't been hard to do, since I pretty much tripped over the starting line), we had known each other for years. Yeah, she made fun of me sometimes. But I also knew I could go to her for help and advice on just about anything.

I even miss the "little punchie-wunchies" I used to get from her when she thought I had said or done something particularly dorky. Actually, that was another reason I wished she were still around: I wanted to ask her if I was getting less dorky. I know that would count as a miracle of some sort, but I've noticed this odd thing happening since we got back: some of the girls – particularly

Rafaella Martinez and Misty Longacres – have started to act as if they actually think I'm a human being or something.

Rafaella has even smiled at me a couple of times.

It's hard to get used to.

As if getting hassled by Jordan and feeling lousy about Linnsy wasn't enough, I was also having a problem with Ms Weintraub. She actually expected Pleskit and me to make up all the classwork we had missed while we were off saving the galaxy!

"Sheesh," I complained. "You'd think a guy could get extra credit in social studies for saving galactic civilization from total collapse."

"I give you all the credit in the world, Tim," said Ms Weintraub. "I still want you to know why the Revolutionary War took place."

"Good luck," snorted Jordan. "He doesn't even know what colour George Washington's white horse was!"

This earned him a laugh from Brad Kent, who I think must have been a dog in a previous life, since that's the only way I can explain his total devotion to Jordan. I always expect him to lick Jordan's face and ask for a biscuit after he barks out one of those pathetic suck-up laughs.

Pleskit had missed as much work as I had, of course. The difference is that he has a truly mighty brain, so he was able to make it up more quickly. Which meant I was the one who ended up staying after school to get extra help.

One Friday afternoon I left school after one of these sessions. It was a beautiful spring day, which was nice, except it was also sort of weird, because it had been winter when we left for Billa Kindikan. I was riding my bike, and when I got to the bridge, I stopped to stare at the embassy for a while. Basically it's a huge flying saucer dangling from the tip of a two-hundred-foot-high hook that thrusts up from the big hill in Thorncraft Park. Even though it's been there since last autumn, I still sometimes think I'm dreaming when I see it – especially since I'm the only kid on Earth who gets to visit it on a regular basis, on account of Pleskit being my best friend.

A light rain started, and I decided I had better get going. But just seconds after I crossed the bridge, a kid I had never seen before jumped out from behind a tree.

I screeched to a halt, barely avoiding crashing into him.

Eyes wild, face desperate, he gasped, "I'm in terrible trouble, Tim! You have to help me!"

2

THE PERILS OF WEALTH

"Okay, Pleskit," said Robert McNally, the Earthling hired to be my bodyguard. "Help me get this straight: if this *urpelli* thing works out, your Fatherly One actually has a chance to become the richest guy in the *galaxy*?"

McNally and I were in the embassy kitchen for an after-school snack. We were discussing what it meant that a previously unknown Grand *Urpelli*

8

had been discovered so close to Earth that it was part of the Fatherly One's trading franchise. I wanted to answer my bodyguard's question, but I had just taken a sip of fizzing *feezlebort*, and my tongue was not yet ready to resume working. So I couldn't explain, again, that an *urpelli* is a sort of hole through time and space.

A Grand *Urpelli* – and the one located near Earth is only the second we know of in the entire galaxy – connects all the rest of them. This makes it sort of a huge central station for faster-than-light travel.

Barvgis, the Fatherly One's round and slimy personal assistant, took up the conversation for me. Plucking an inch-long squirmer from the bowl in front of him, he held it up and said, "Pretend this squirmer represents all the money possessed by the Earthling known as Bill Gates."

McNally nodded. "Okay. I'm pretending."

"Good," said Barvgis. Ignoring the squirmer's tiny screams and frantically wriggling legs, he tossed it into his mouth. He chewed once, swallowed, then burped in satisfaction. Patting his stomach proudly, he said, "Now, if that represented the current fortune of Bill Gates, the *potential* fortune Meenom could earn from the Grand *Urpelli* would engulf it as easily as my vast and mighty stomach engulfed that squirmer." Bargvis belched contentedly, then said proudly, "My stomach, by the way, has been known to contain *thousands* of squirmers."

McNally shook his head. "It's hard to imagine anyone having that much money."

"It's certainly hard to imagine *my* Fatherly One having that much," I said, now that the *feezlebort* had released its grip on my tongue.

"I think your Fatherly One is having a hard time imagining it, too," said Barvgis. He shovelled more squirmers into his mouth, then clamped his lips shut and began using one of his thick, blunt fingers to poke in the squirmer parts that were still sticking out.

"That's one reason the ambassador has asked me to stay on for a while longer," said *Wakkam* Akkim, the birdlike being who serves as the Fatherly One's spiritual massage master.

"You're staying?" I asked happily. "I thought

your visit was temporary."

"Yeah," said McNally. "I thought you had only stayed this long because Meenom was so distraught while Tim and Pleskit were lost on Billa Kindikan."

The *wakkam* waggled her feathery brows at us. "That was the main reason to stay. But yesterday the ambassador asked me to become a permanent staff member."

Barvgis swallowed, belched, then said sincerely, "Wonderful news! Care to explain the ambassador's reasons?"

"Gladly," said the *wakkam*. "Pleskit's Fatherly One is concerned about the danger a sudden influx of incredible wealth poses to one's spiritual wellbeing."

"What's wrong with sudden wealth?" asked McNally. "I think I could handle that kind of problem!"

The *wakkam* smiled. "Money is like gravity. Life would be hard without it. But in excess it can pull things out of their established orbit, twist and contort their shapes, even cause them to crash and burn."

"So you're saying money is bad?" I asked, feeling puzzled.

She waggled her feathery brows. "As *Wakkam* Faluda puts it, 'The only thing worse than having money is not having it!' "

I wanted to ask more about this, but just then the dreaded Ms Buttsman, who has a personality like a *grindlezark*, stalked in. "Your Fatherly One wishes to see you, Pleskit," she said. "You, too, *Mr* McNally."

Then she smiled – a pleasant expression when seen on the face of most human beings but utterly terrifying when displayed on the face of Ms Buttsman.

McNally sighed. The two of us got to our feet and headed for the Fatherly One's office.

We found him floating about five feet above the floor in his command pod, tapping commands into the keypads on the armrests. The command pod has a well-padded chair surrounded by a clear blue shell that curves around and over it, with a two-foot-wide opening in the front. It should be a relaxing place to work. However, I don't think the Fatherly One *ever* truly relaxes, in the pod or anywhere else.

When he noticed us, he moved his *sphen-gnut-ksher* in a gesture that meant he wanted us to wait while he finished what he was doing. I interpreted this for McNally, who nodded and stood in silence, hands behind his back, feet slightly apart. He looked calm and relaxed. Despite the relaxed look, I knew that even in this seemingly safe place, he was ready to spring into action instantly should any threat arise.

The Fatherly One farted a signal to the command pod. It floated slowly to the floor. He stepped out and said, "I need to speak seriously with both of you."

Uh-oh, I thought, wondering what I had done now.

He led us to the Alcove of Intimacy, a small space at the back of his office used for private conferences. Twisting a knob mounted on the wall, he adjusted the table to make it the right size for three beings to have a private conversation.

We took our places. Face solemn, the Fatherly

One said, "I know you are both aware that the stakes regarding our mission here on Earth have risen enormously."

"We were just discussing that, sir," said McNally.

"Let me see if I can make the situation clearer," said the Fatherly One. "This Grand *Urpelli* is one of the most significant discoveries in the history of galactic commerce. Many groups would like to control it, and there is much anger that it chanced to be included in an obscure franchise for a minor planet. Of course, it is universally agreed that unexpected rewards are one of the joys of being an entrepreneur. But sums of money this vast can change people's opinions – warp them, almost."

I thought of *Wakkam* Akkim comparing money to gravity.

"Some of our past troubles make sense now that we know others were already aware of the *urpelli* and wanted to have me removed from my position before I became aware of it as well. Now that the *urpelli* is public knowledge, the challenges to my authority will continue, perhaps even increase." He put his hands flat on the table. "We must not give our challengers *any* reason to claim I am not capable of handling the franchise."

He turned to McNally. "Please understand that, while I greatly desire to protect my financial position, this is not just about personal wealth. With the discovery of the second Grand *Urpelli*, Earth has become the main topic of conversation across the Milky Way, from beings in the street to the top levels of power. Because your planet still ranks as barely civilized—"

McNally started to object, but the Fatherly One raised a hand. "Please, Mr McNally, take no offence. You know the reasons as well as I do. A planet with so much war, hunger, racism, and environmental degradation cannot possibly be called civilized. Even so, I believe Earth could be truly wonderful if you can only overcome the things holding you back. Many beings of power and prominence disagree; they see the planet merely as a place to be exploited."

He paused and took a deep breath. "Now, the reason I called you in – called you *both* in," he stressed, turning to look directly at me, "is to inform you that an official galactic inspection team will be arriving soon to look over our operations. We must not provide them with *any* excuse to revoke the Earth franchise." He turned back to McNally. "You have been protecting my childling, Mr McNally. Now I ask you to protect me as well."

"In what way, sir?"

"I need to be shielded from Pleskit's occasionally rash actions. Foolish behaviour on his part could be very costly – not just for me but for the entire planet."

"I'll do what I can, Mr Ambassador. But keeping Pleskit and Tim in line is like herding cats."

"You are not responsible for Tim," the Fatherly One said sharply.

McNally nodded. "I'm glad we're clear on that. But unless you ban Pleskit from seeing him, the two of them *are* going to be together."

I cringed inside. Why did McNally have to say this?

"You bring up a difficult subject," said the

Fatherly One. "I have already concluded that for the present it would be a good idea to limit the time Tim and Pleskit spend together."

"Fatherly One!" I cried.

He farted a command for silence. "It may also be time to reconsider my decision to send you to school outside the embassy, Pleskit. I fear we have reached a point where the dangers of public exposure outweigh the benefits."

I stared at him in horror. It had taken me months to learn to fit in at my new school. Now I had friends, and I felt as if I belonged. "You can't do this to me!" I cried.

The Fatherly One's answer came in a voice that was hard and cold. "I will do what is necessary."

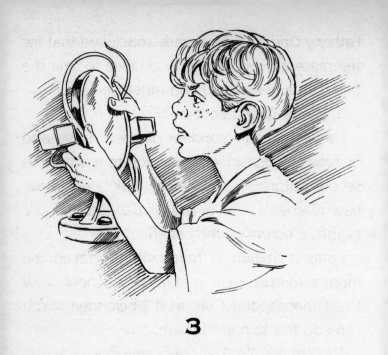

3

ILLEGAL ALIEN

I like to help people well enough, but with all that's happened in the last few months, I'm more suspicious than I used to be. So I didn't say anything right away, just studied the kid for a minute. He was a little taller than me, athletic-looking, with dark hair, big eyes, and a face that would have been right at home in one of those dweeby bands girls are always going nuts for. At least, it would have if it hadn't been all twisted up with panic.

"What do you want?" I asked cautiously.

"I need to meet the alien kid."

I sighed. I'm so used to being friends with Pleskit, I sometimes forget that almost everyone else on the planet is dying to meet the aliens. "Sorry," I said. "Can't be arranged."

"But I *have* to talk to him!" cried the kid, gripping the handlebars of my bike as if they were a life preserver.

I was starting to get nervous. "What's the deal?" I asked. "Are you just an alien groupie – or are

you working for some multinational corporation that wants to put Pleskit's face on their cereal boxes?"

He shook his head. "No, no, it's nothing like that! I swear. I've just got to meet him."

I actually had some sympathy, since I would have felt the same way if I hadn't been lucky enough to be in the school Pleskit got assigned to. But I also knew how many people were trying to get at my friend, and how stressful it was for him.

"Sorry," I said again. "Can't happen."

The kid burst into tears. "*You don't understand!*"

"No, *you* don't understand," I snapped, wrenching my handlebars out of his grasp. "You'll have to find some other way to meet him."

I started to pedal away.

The kid ran after me and grabbed my elbow. I tried to pull myself free, but he was surprisingly strong.

"You *really* don't understand," he said. "My name is Beebo. Beebo Frimbat. I'm an extraterrestrial, like Pleskit. I'm stranded, and I need help."

Not long ago I would have at least listened to

someone who claimed he was an alien, no matter how crazy it might have seemed. But that was before so many reporters and businesspeople started trying to use me to get to Pleskit. "If you're an alien, then I'm Conan the Barbarian," I said, disgusted that he thought I would fall for such a stupid story.

"I'll prove it!" he said angrily.

"What are you going to do? Peel off your face?"

It was his turn to be disgusted. "Don't be so dramatic." He glanced around, then pointed at a near-by branch that was lying on the ground.

"Watch this!"

He wiggled his finger.

The branch floated into the air.

"You've got a friend in the tree pulling it up," I said, a little desperately.

The kid made a flicking motion with his finger. The branch went tumbling across the grass.

"So much for the friend-in-the-tree theory," he said smugly. "Now do you believe me?"

I just stood there, gaping.

"I said, 'Now do you believe me?'"

"Yeah, I guess I do," I muttered.

Suddenly the situation had become far more confusing. Even though the kid's demonstration of telekinetic powers was enough to convince me what he was saying was true, I still wasn't sure I should help him. That felt weird, since helping an alien in distress had been one of my prime daydreams from the time I was in kindergarten. But I had already lived out that dream by helping Pleskit. In the process I had spent more time than I would have liked being terrorized by aliens who wanted to suck out my brains and stuff like that. So I wasn't quite as eager for something like this as I would have been BP (Before Pleskit).

"Okay," I said slowly, "I believe you're an alien. But what do you need *me* for? Why don't you just contact the embassy yourself?"

The boy looked horrified. "I can't do that!"

"Why not?"

"Because I'm an *illegal* alien."

"Huh?"

"I don't belong here," he said, speaking slowly, as if he thought I was some kind of an idiot. "I will be glad to tell you the entire story, but *not* while we are standing out in the open."

Well, I was still kind of nervous about all this. But the kid seemed truly distressed. And he was just a kid, after all.

At least, he seemed to be.

"All right," I said slowly. "You'd better come home with me."

He broke into a huge smile. "Thank you! You may have just saved my life!"

That made me nervous all over again. "Is someone out to get you?"

"No, no. At least, I don't think so. Come on, let's go!"

So I took him back to my apartment. Mom was still at work, which made things a little easier. As I opened the door, my Veeblax scampered over, yeeping as it came. It sniffed at the kid suspiciously, then climbed on to my shoulder and changed its shape so it looked like a rock, which was something it did whenever it wanted to hide.

The kid laughed. "I did not know you had shapeshifters on Earth!"

"We don't. This is a Veeblax. They come from

Hevi-Hevi. I raised this one from an *oog-slama* that Pleskit gave me."

"Can we contact Pleskit now?" the kid said eagerly.

"Tell me your story first."

"It will be easier to tell you both at once. I've already proved I'm not from this world. If you're still worried, remember that Pleskit won't come without his bodyguard. So you'll have plenty of protection."

"How do you know about his bodyguard?" I asked, suddenly suspicious again.

The kid looked at me in disbelief. "Everyone on your planet knows about Pleskit and his bodyguard! I *can* read a newspaper, you know."

"Okay, okay. No need to get so cranky."

"Sorry. I am just extremely nervous."

"All right, you stay here. I'll go contact Pleskit. Uh, do you want something to eat while you wait?"

"That would be nice. I'm hungrier than a *paznak*."

I made him a baloney sandwich then went to

call Pleskit on the special comm-device he had given me.

Unfortunately, it was not Pleskit who answered – it was the dreaded Ms Buttsman.

She looked unusually happy, which made me nervous.

My nervousness only increased when she said, "Ah, Mr Tompkins! I'm afraid I have some rather unpleasant news for you. Ambassador Meenom has decided that you and Pleskit make a dangerous combination, so he has asked me to disconnect the direct line the two of you have been using to communicate." She smiled gleefully. "Sorry, Timbo!"

Then the screen went blank.

She must have left the sound on for a moment longer, because her laughter lingered in the air even after her face was gone.

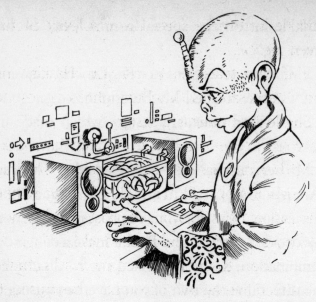

4

EARGON FOOZ

As McNally and I left the office of the Fatherly One, his secretary Beezle Whompis flickered into sight. Beezle Whompis is an energy being. He's usually invisible and only takes physical form as a convenience for the rest of us. I noticed that he was flickering a little around the edges and wondered if he was tired. It wouldn't be surprising. Everyone in the embassy has been working very hard since the discovery of the Grand *Urpelli*.

"I've been meaning to tell you, Pleskit," he said, "these snacks Maktel brought as a guesting gift are extraordinarily pleasing."

He reached into the bag holding the snacks and pulled out a glowing blue sphere. The bag was nearly empty, but given how long it had been since Maktel's visit, Beezle Whompis was clearly working to make the snacks last.

He tossed the sphere, which was actually condensed energy, into his mouth. I heard a loud *zap*! Instantly, he was surrounded by crackling blue light.

"Ah," said Beezle Whompis. "I needed that!"

"That reminds me," said McNally. "I could use a cup of coffee."

I smiled. "I'm sure Shhh-foop would be glad to prepare one for you."

McNally groaned. "Don't even mention it to her!" he ordered.

I tried not to laugh. Despite Shhh-foop's wondrous skills as a cook, for some reason our queen of the kitchen has yet to master the art of making a simple cup of coffee. Her continued failure in this matter has caused her much emotional distress. McNally, to his credit, has been willing to sample every new experiment, despite the often disastrous results she achieves. But it was nothing he tried to encourage, and I could tell he just wanted to slip away for a while.

"You need to go anywhere, Pleskit?" he asked.

"No," I said. "I am going to stay here and brood about what the Fatherly One said. I am most disturbed by the possibility of being pulled out of school."

"I'm not wild about the idea, either," said McNally. "You'll still need a bodyguard, I suppose, so it's not like I'll lose my job. But it's going to be awfully boring if we spend most of our time stuck in the embassy."

Though he did not say it, I suspected one of the reasons McNally did not want to stop going to my classroom was that he enjoyed seeing our beautiful teacher, Ms Weintraub, every day.

"I am going to go seek the advice of the Grandfatherly One," I said.

"Good idea. I've got some reports to do, but I'm gonna slip out for a cup of Joe first. See you later, kid."

I like it when McNally calls me "kid". It feels friendly and comfortable.

I went to the chamber where we keep the brain of the Grandfatherly One.

I was surprised to find Eargon Fooz already there.

Though I am used to many forms of beings, for some reason Eargon Fooz's horselike body seemed oddly confined in this room. Perhaps it was because I first knew her as a creature of the jungles. Her tribe follows a way that is close to nature, using only the most simple tools to build homes that are little more than shelters from wind and rain. They live this way not because they could not do better but simply because they think it is a good way to exist.

She is strong but gentle, and she had saved our lives on Billa Kindikan. Unfortunately, she had been banned from her own tribe because she had been kidnapped and taken into the forbidden city of Ilbar-Fakkam by one of Mikta-makta-mookta's thugs. She could return to her people only after a year of "purification" had passed. The Fatherly One had invited her to live with us during this time – which seemed the least we could do, considering that she would never have been banished if she hadn't tried to help us.

When she saw me enter, she extended the humanoid arms that grow from her shoulders. It was a graceful gesture of greeting, and her beautiful four-eyed face showed true pleasure at my arrival.

"Greetings, Pleskit," she said, speaking in Standard Galactic.

"Greetings, Eargon Fooz. How are you today?"

"How do you think she is?" snapped the Grandfatherly One, speaking through one of the tubes that extend from the tank where we have kept his brain since he died. "She misses her kids and her home. By the way, greetings, whippersnapper."

"Greetings, O Venerated One."

As I spoke I placed a friendly hand on Eargon

Fooz's shoulder. The smooth skin had grown dark to match the room, but quickly turned purple around my hand.

"We were discussing whether I should go somewhere else on your planet to live until it is time for my return to Billa Kindikan," said Eargon Fooz. "I am missing the feel of sun on my back, the smell and buzz of the jungle." She turned her head away. "But mostly I am missing my younglings."

I felt terrible. Eargon Fooz would still be home on Billa Kindikan if she hadn't done so much to help us.

"We should discuss this with the Fatherly One," I said.

"Hah!" snorted the Grandfatherly One. "Try to find time to discuss *anything* with Mr Hotshot Ambassador now that he's ready to build the biggest fortune in the galaxy."

"I just had a discussion with him," I said defensively.

"Let me guess," said the Grandfatherly One. "Was it about how he wants you not to cause any trouble now that we're under such intense scrutiny? Did you discuss anything *you* wanted to talk about?"

My Venerated Ancestor can be uncomfortably perceptive on occasion. "You are correct," I said reluctantly. "In fact, the Fatherly One has suggested that perhaps I should leave my school and pursue my studies here in the embassy."

"Brilliant!" said the Grandfatherly One. "Then you can be as lonely and isolated as I am."

"And I," said Eargon Fooz mournfully.

"Look," said the Grandfatherly One. "Your Fatherly One has a lot on his mind, and a lot at stake. It's reasonable for him to ask you to be careful. It's *not* reasonable for him to expect you to curl up and hibernate. And it's not good for him to set aside his own ideas and beliefs merely for the sake of a vast and enormous fortune."

The words of the Grandfatherly One were still ringing in my ears when I returned to my room and found that the comm-device I use to communicate with Tim was missing.

I ran to Ms Buttsman's desk. She was busy adjusting her hair.

"If you're wondering what happened to your comm-device," she said, not even looking at me, "I took it out of your room."

"WHY?"

"Your Fatherly One suggested it might be better if you and that Tompkins boy were not in such constant communication. He fears you make a bad combination."

I farted in disgust and stalked away. I could not believe the Fatherly One was trying to cut me off from my best friend in this way. So perhaps I was not in the most rational state of mind when I went to one of the embassy's Earth-style phones to call Tim. If I had been, I might have been more cautious when he picked up the receiver at his end and cried, "Pleskit! Thank goodness it's you! I need you to get over here, quick! We've got a . . . situation."

"What kind of situation?" I asked nervously.

"I can't explain. I just need to see you. Quick!"

5

ETHICAL CONFUSION

I was torn by Tim's call. I did not want to get into a situation that would cost us the chance to become the richest family in the galaxy. But when a friend calls for help, what kind of friend are you if you don't go?

Confused and troubled, I went to seek McNally, whom I needed to find before I could go to Tim's anyway.

My bodyguard was not in his room, and I was worried that he had not yet returned from getting his coffee. Since there had been no plans for going out that afternoon, he was technically off-duty. Had he gone to see one of his lady friends? I wondered if he might be visiting Ms Weintraub. He *had* brought her to the big embassy party that had ended up with Tim, Maktel, Linnsy, and me getting accidentally snatched from Earth.

I burped an information request into the box mounted next to McNally's door.

After a brief humming sound the box said, "Mr McNally is currently in the presence of your Venerated Ancestor, Ventrah Komquist."

I hurried back to the Grandfatherly One's chambers. Eargon Fooz had left. McNally was sitting at a small table, a cardboard cup filled with coffee on the floor next to him. He and my Venerated Ancestor were playing an Earthling game called draughts.

"Back so soon, sproutling?" said the Grandfatherly One.

"I need to speak to my bodyguard."

"Well, speak," said the Grandfatherly One. "Nothing you should be saying to him that I shouldn't be able to hear."

I was beginning to feel a distinct lack of privacy.

"I have had an emergency message from Tim," I said. "He urgently requests our presence at his apartment."

"Aw, geez, Pleskit," said McNally. "Your Fatherly One just got done asking us to stay out of trouble!"

"I did not go looking for trouble," I replied. "It seems to have found me on its own. Actually, I am not even certain we should go."

"Abandon a friend in a time of need, and you can stop coming to visit me," said the Grandfatherly One sharply.

"But you know the Fatherly One's wishes," I said, feeling confused.

"Yeah, yeah, yeah. Well, we don't always get what we wish for, do we? I already told you, your Fatherly One is getting a little out of control. Now, pack me up and let's get going."

"Pack you up?" asked McNally nervously.

"You heard me," snapped the Grandfatherly

One. "I'm going with you. Come on, let's get a move on."

McNally still hesitated.

"Tim did sound most perturbed," I said.

McNally sighed. "I may be risking my job here."

"That's why I want you to bring me along," said the Grandfatherly One. "My presence will give you a degree of coverage for your actions. Think of me as a living insurance policy."

"But you're dead," I pointed out.

"Don't be such a *seekl-fingus*," snapped the Grandfatherly One. "You understand the point."

"I guess so," said McNally, though he didn't sound entirely convinced.

It took us a few minutes to transfer the Grandfatherly One's brain into the Brain Transport Device. A few minutes after that we were heading down the tube to the garage where the limousine is parked.

Ralph-the-driver looked slightly startled when he saw McNally carrying the Grandfatherly One. But he didn't say anything. He never does.

We piled into the limousine, and Ralph drove us to Tim's apartment building.

"Thank goodness you're here!" said Tim when we showed up at his door. "Hey, you brought the Grandfatherly One! Cool!"

The Grandfatherly One extended the speaking tubes from his BTD. "Greetings, Earthling whippersnapper," he said. "Nice to see you again. Now, what's this little emergency you've got on your hands?"

Tim pointed to a nice-looking boy standing in the kitchen doorway. He seemed to be about our age, though he was a little taller than either of us.

"What's his problem?" asked McNally suspiciously.

Tim leaned closer and said softly, "He's not an Earthling."

"Uh-oh," said the Grandfatherly One. He turned his viewing devices directly toward the boy. "That's a pretty big claim, youngster. You ready to prove it?"

The boy bit his lip, then said, "I think it's time I showed you my true face."

"Dang it!" cried Tim. "When I said something

about taking your face off, you accused me of being overly dramatic!"

"It's not my face I'm going to take off," said the boy. He walked over to the dining-room table and stopped in front of it, standing with his back to it. Then he stripped off his shirt.

"What's he going to do?" muttered Tim nervously. "Show us some weird alien body part?"

Before I could answer, the boy stopped cold, freezing as if he had turned into one of those dummies the Earthlings use to display clothing in their department stores.

"Has he gone into *kleptra*?" Tim asked nervously.

"Wait a second," I said, holding up a hand and farting the fart of nervousness. "Keep watching."

We heard a hissing from the boy's body.

McNally stepped up next to me and moved into a protective stance. "He's not going to explode or anything, is he?" he asked tensely.

"Admirable to be on your guard, McNally," said the Grandfatherly One. "But it's nothing like

that. Even so, you'd better be the first one to go around back."

"Around back?" asked McNally.

"Back of the kid," said the Grandfatherly One, sounding exasperated.

Moving cautiously, McNally walked around to the other side of the table, so he was standing behind Beebo.

Tim and I followed him.

"Great galloping galaxies," I whispered as a small door swung down from the boy's bare back. "He was wearing a bodysuit!"

The door stretched down until it touched the table, forming a kind of ramp. The surface – the part that had been *inside* the boy – was covered with what looked like circuits.

A cloud of steam, or smoke, or something, puffed out from the opening. Then a small orange face appeared in the doorway.

6

THE STRANDING OF BEEBO

Ducking, but only a little, because he was no more than two feet tall, the alien climbed out of the now frozen body. He had a turned-up nose and oversized dark eyes and was so cute that it was hard not to go "Awwww" as soon as you saw him.

"Greetings!" he said. "My name is Beebo. Beebo Frimbat, Prince of Roogbat!"

Three antennae grew in a triangular formation on Beebo's head – one front and centre, the other two about halfway back. An odd combination of hair and scales came forward around the central antenna to make a pair of points that ended just above his eyebrows.

Beebo's ears were oversized, too, and slightly pointy. His feet were somewhat birdlike, with two toes in front and one in back – something you could see because his soft leather "boots" were open front and back to let the toes stick out.

He walked slowly down the ramp. Once he was standing on the table, he made a sweeping bow.

"Are you really a prince?" asked Pleskit.

"I most certainly am!" said Beebo, drawing himself up to his full height – which still wouldn't have brought him anywhere near my waist if he had been standing on the floor.

"You look sort of like an elf," I said. "Or maybe an elf from outer space."

Part of the reason for this was his costume, a two-piece outfit that looked like it belonged to some fantasy forest creature.

"Cuteness is a virtue," Beebo replied, stretching

so hard that his joints made little popping sounds. "*Wowza-yoicks!* It feels good to get out of that suit. I was really cramped in there!"

"What are you doing here?" asked the Grandfatherly One.

"Here with you or here on Earth?" he asked.

"Both!"

"It's a long story."

"Better start talking," growled McNally.

Since it seemed easier to let Beebo stay where he was, the rest of us sat down at the table, which made sort of a stage for him. Putting his hands behind his back, he began to pace, stepping over the salt and pepper shakers, walking around the napkin holder. Finally he sat down on a stack of my textbooks.

"It started as a school project," he said.

"What kind of school do you go to?" I asked in surprise.

"Oh, it's a lovely school! We have a lot of laughter. That's our school motto: 'Life is a joke, and then you die.' Anyway, one of the things we have to do to graduate is study humour on other planets. Well, that and figure out how to survive while we're visiting that planet. Our elders believe that learning to survive in a primitive and hostile environment furthers our journey to maturity."

"Maturity's not all it's cracked up to be," muttered the Grandfatherly One.

"Sharp, but only moderately funny," said Beebo. "I give it a three."

"On a scale of what?" demanded the Grandfatherly One.

Beebo grinned, which was so cute it made you want to smile just seeing it. "One to fifty. One is about equal to a small twitch at the corner of the mouth. Fifty is when you laugh so hard you die and return to the arms of the Great Jester who made us all."

"Whippersnapper," muttered the Grandfatherly One.

"Why don't you just get on with the story?" said McNally.

Beebo looked uncomfortable. "When the supervisors drop us off, they are supposed to monitor our survival. They want us to be tested, but they prefer us not to die, an event that tends to distress a Parental Unit. However, my supervisors have disappeared! I went to the pick-up site, and they did not show up. That was nearly two weeks ago. I have tried all the normal methods of contacting them, with no success. During that time I have been making my way to Syracuse in the hope that I might contact Pleskit. I had read about him, and I hoped he might be willing to help me. But the embassy is very securely guarded. It was not easy to get to you, Pleskit. That was why I accosted Tim in the park today."

"Well, I'm glad you finally reached me," said Pleskit soothingly. "We'll take you straight back to the embassy. The Fatherly One will have this solved in less than a day."

Beebo looked alarmed, and a complicated series of expressions flitted across his face. I could identify guilt, fear, shame, and sorrow. It is likely there were other feelings being expressed as well, ones I was not aware of, since Pleskit has told me that many species have emotions unique to themselves.

"Please don't!" he cried in horror. "I can't go to the embassy. Please, please don't make me do that!"

With those big eyes and that charming face, when Beebo looked so distraught you wanted to do everything you could to make things better. He looked like a kitten that had just lost its mother.

"What is the problem?" asked Pleskit, looking baffled.

Beebo glanced around nervously, then whispered, "Roogbat is a non-trading planet."

"Uh-oh," said the Grandfatherly One.

"What does that have to do with anything?" I asked.

"Beebo's planet is not recognized by the Trading Federation," said the Grandfatherly One. "Therefore, the embassy is prohibited from helping him. In fact, if Pleskit's Fatherly One were to become aware that Beebo is here on Earth, he would be honour-bound to turn the boy over to the Trading Federation for disciplinary action."

McNally looked at the Grandfatherly One curiously. "Don't you have the same obligation, sir?"

The Grandfatherly One just laughed. "One of the few benefits of being dead is that I am no longer bound by foolish restrictions. Neither are you, McNally, in case you were wondering, since Earth is not yet a member of the Federation." He swung his viewing tubes and speaking extensions towards Beebo. "But you have something to explain, sproutling – namely, what in the name of the Seven Moons of Skatwag possessed your advisers to bring you to Earth if your own world is not part of the Trading Federation?"

"They didn't realize this planet was a Federation franchise when they made the assignment," said Beebo. "Remember, you haven't been here all that long yourselves."

"I suppose that makes sense," grumbled the Grandfatherly One. "But it doesn't change the problem."

"Just what *is* the problem?" asked Pleskit.

The Grandfatherly One made a noise like clearing his throat – sort of an odd thing to do, since he doesn't have a throat. I think he just does it to gain time while he's thinking.

"All right," he said at last. "Here's what you need to know. The dominant legal body in the galaxy is the Interplanetary Trading Federation.

You're well aware of that. What you may not be aware of is that not all eligible planets choose to join the Federation."

"Why not?" asked Pleskit, who was clearly startled by this information.

"They don't want to accept the restrictions that come with membership. The Federation is relatively fierce about this, and such planets are cut off from contact with the larger galaxy. They are not allowed to trade with member planets – not allowed to have any contact with them at all, in fact."

"Whoa," I said. "That's harsh!"

"Galaxywide civilizations aren't built by sissies," said the Grandfatherly One. "Besides, the fact that something is prohibited doesn't mean it's not going to happen. In fact, the restriction on trading between Federation members and non-trading planets virtually guarantees a black market."

"A what?" I asked.

" 'Black market' refers to any trading that occurs outside legal structures. One reason power – and by 'power' I mean the ruling structure in a society

– likes to make things illegal is that it provides a tool for controlling people."

"Now you've got *me* puzzled," said McNally.

"It's like this. If you make something that is popular and not really harmful illegal, then you can be sure some beings are going to do it anyway. Since it's not really harmful, the authorities can ignore it if they want. But it gives them a handy way to take action against a being or group they find troublesome." He shook his speaking tubes in disgust. "It's all a vast and nasty game. Anyway, the point is planets that have decided not to join the Federation are diplomatically and socially cut off from the main body of the galaxy. We don't have physical battles with them – we've all grown beyond *that*, thank the stars. But the Federation has some pretty harsh policies for Traders who deal with non-Federation planets." He turned his speaking tubes directly toward Beebo. "And for non-Federation travellers who intrude on Federation planets!"

"So what, specifically, does that all mean for us?" asked McNally.

"It means two things. First, Beebo doesn't

belong here, because Earth is now linked to the Trading Federation through Meenom's franchise. Second, if Meenom were found to be sheltering him, he could have his franchise stripped from him."

Pleskit groaned. "This is exactly the kind of thing the Fatherly One feared!"

"What about Beebo?" I asked.

"He can be arrested for his intrusion," said the Grandfatherly One grimly.

Beebo gave a squawk of terror.

7

A DESPERATE PLEA FOR SHELTER

I was startled by the things the Grandfatherly One told us. Startled and troubled. The powers running the galaxy were not as benevolent as I had been led to believe in the early stages of my education.

Obviously, I was faced with a difficult moral dilemma: should I turn Beebo in or try to help him get back to his own people?

My instinct was to try to help him get home. But it hadn't even been two hours since the Fatherly One had asked me not to cause any more trouble. And I was in no hurry to endanger our chances of becoming the richest family unit in the galaxy.

But I knew what it was like to be stranded on a planet far from home. Had not Tim, Maktel, Linnsy, and I been in exactly that situation only a few weeks ago ourselves? We never would have survived if Eargon Fooz had not helped us. She had acted without concern for what it might cost her. And look what the cost had been: exile from her home and family.

Could I do less for another traveller in need?

Beebo must have seen me hesitating, because he flung himself on to my chest, wrapped his legs around me, put his little hands on my cheeks and his little orange face close to mine, and cried. "Don't turn me in, Mr Pleskit! Oh, please, please, please, please, please, don't turn me in. Who knows what they'll do to me? Who knows what will become of me? Just help me find my way home. That's all I ask, all I want, all I long for.

Help me find my way home!"

Tim, McNally, and the Grandfatherly One burst out laughing.

"Let go of me, Beebo!" I said, struggling to disentangle myself from his grasp.

"Sorry," he said, jumping back to the table. "Didn't mean to distress you. But will you help me?"

Common sense said, *You've got to be kidding*. Wisdom said, *This is a bad idea*. Basic intelligence said, *Run away, run away!*

But the memory of my own recent troubles, plus the desperate look in Beebo's enormous and appealing eyes, urged me to set those things aside and help.

"What do you think, McNally?" I asked.

My bodyguard looked distressed. "I don't know, Pleskit. The whole reason I went into this business was to protect people. But your Fatherly One is going to toast my butt if I let you get in trouble over this. And, frankly, my main job is to watch out for *you*. I'm not sure what to do." He turned to the Grandfatherly One. "What do you think, Ventrah?"

The Grandfatherly One snorted. "I think if you help him, odds are good you're going to get into big trouble. I think you're probably going to do it anyway. I also think that's probably just as well, since I wouldn't give two *wizzikki* for you or the sproutling if you didn't help him."

I took a deep breath. "All right, we will help you, Beebo. But since you don't want to go to the embassy, how exactly do you want us to help?"

"I need shelter. And I would like you to try to contact my people for me."

"Can't do it from the embassy," said the Grandfatherly One. "A message sent to someplace like Roogbat would show up on the records. Actually, it would be hard to get such a message through the *urpelli* system by standard means. You're going to have to get someone outside the system to carry it for you."

"Is there a black market for communications?" I asked.

"I'm sure there is," said the Grandfatherly One. "Unfortunately, I have no idea right now how to get in touch with it."

I turned to Tim. "Obviously we cannot take Beebo back to the embassy. Can he stay with you for the time being?"

"How am I supposed to explain him to my mother?"

I smiled. "You've explained weirder stuff."

He smiled back. "Yeah, I guess I have. Okay, I think I can handle it."

"*Feezle dee-goopus!*" cried Beebo. "Thank you, thank both of you. Thank *all* of you! I will be no problem, you won't regret this, you'll be extraordinarily happy you chose to help me."

I was not entirely sure that was true. And I could see that Tim was starting to wonder about it already.

"I should probably return to my bodysuit before your mother arrives," said Beebo. "It will be easier to explain things if she sees me in human form first."

He climbed the ramp into the artificial body and pulled the door up behind him.

We all stood there, watching.

The suit didn't move.

Tim looked at me nervously.

"Beebo?" I called. "Are you all right?"

Before I could say anything else, the door in the bodysuit opened again. Beebo came hurtling down the ramp.

"It's broken!" he cried, his huge eyes wide with horror. "The suit is *broken*!"

8

THE WHIRLWIND

Beebo stood for a second, quivering with terror. Then he clapped his hands to the sides of his head and began to spin around, making a high, wailing sound.

"Quiet!" I said sharply. "Next thing you know, the neighbours will be at the door, wanting to know what's going on!"

Beebo stopped squalling. Instead he stood in

58

place and started to vibrate.

Soon he was moving so fast he nearly disappeared.

Suddenly the mug on the table next to him floated into the air. It began to move faster, heading on a collision course with the wall behind him. McNally lunged across the floor and snatched it just before it hit. But other things were starting to float, too – books, the jacket I had dropped on the floor the day before and never picked up, pencils, the telephone, potted plants, my backpack. The faster Beebo vibrated, the more things went into the air. They began swirling around him, as if he were the centre of a small tornado.

"Hey!" cried the Grandfatherly One, as his BTD floated into the air. "Cut that out, Beebo!"

A moment later the Veeblax flew into the air, eeping desperately.

McNally dived across the table and wrapped his hands around Beebo's waist. That slowed him down a little – partly because some of his energy was being transferred to McNally, who also started to shake.

"W-w-w-ill you c-c-c-c-cut tha-t-t-t out-t-t-t!" cried the bodyguard.

He wasn't stammering because he was afraid. He was just having a hard time getting the words out because he was shaking so hard.

Suddenly a blast of energy shot out of Pleskit's *sphen-gnut-ksher* and zapped into Beebo. He sighed and collapsed into McNally's arms with a blissful smile on his little orange face.

Everything that had been swirling around him clattered to the floor – including the Veeblax and the Grandfatherly One's BTD.

I scooped up the Veeblax, which squawked and wrapped itself around my neck, and raced to the BTD.

"Are you all right?" I cried.

"Yeah, yeah, I'm fine," said the Grandfatherly One. "This thing is designed to withstand a lot of impact. How's McNally?"

"I'm okay," growled the bodyguard, setting Beebo gently on to the table. "Just a little shaken up."

"I'm fine, too," said Beebo dreamily.

Pleskit was sitting on the floor, his back against

the wall. Using his *sphen-gnut-ksher* to send someone into *kling-kphut* is a huge energy drain and always exhausts him.

Then, just to make things perfect, my mother walked through the door.

McNally moved fast when he heard her coming. Snatching up Beebo, he tucked him behind his back. "*Quiet!*" I heard him whisper.

He had time to do this without my mother noticing because she was stunned by the mess Beebo's whirlwind had made out of the living room – not surprising, since it was pretty spectacular, even by my standards.

"Tim," she said, using her best don't-give-me-any-nonsense voice. "Just *what* is going on here?"

Before I could answer, she spotted Beebo's bodysuit, standing empty-eyed and motionless but otherwise looking totally human.

"What is *that?*" she shrieked.

Then she saw Pleskit slumped against the wall. "*And what's wrong with him?*"

She was starting to sound really panicky.

"Mom, Mom, it's nothing serious," I said, trying to sound soothing. "Why don't you sit down? You must be tired from work. I'll make you a cup of tea, and then we can explain everything."

"Skip the tea," said Mom, staying right where she was. "And skip the baloney, too. Just tell me what's going on here."

If I had been missing Linnsy before, I really missed her right then. No one could handle Mom in a situation like this the way she could. But Linnsy wasn't here, so it was up to me.

"I still think you'd better sit down," I said. "Here, let me get you a chair."

While I was fiddling with the chair, I noticed McNally step back towards the hall. He must have dropped off Beebo, because when he stepped forward again he had his hands free.

"All right," said Mom firmly, once she was sitting. "Talk!"

We started to tell her the story of what had happened that afternoon, all talking at once.

"Wait!" she said, holding up her hands. "Wait! One at a time. You first, buster."

She was pointing at me.

When I was about halfway through my story,

she said, "Before you go any further, I want to meet this kid."

Beebo must have been listening, because he instantly came scooting out of the hall, crying, "Pleased to meet you, Mrs Tompkins!"

9

THE ALIEN WHO CAME TO DINNER

Mom burst out laughing. "You are the cutest thing I've seen since Tim was a baby!"

"*Mom!*" I cried in horror.

"Oh, shush, Tim. How you brutes could have even thought about sending this poor little fellow to some kind of galactic foster home is beyond me. He'll stay right here with us until we can find out what happened to his people."

"Boy," I said bitterly, "that wasn't what you said the last time I brought home a puppy."

Mom scowled at me. "Puppies aren't people, Tim. Besides, you've got a Veeblax now, so I think we can stop having the pet argument, okay? Would you like some dinner, Beebo? It sounds like you've had a rough day."

I looked at her in astonishment. Was she going to let us off the hook for the mess?

"Pleskit, McNally, you can stay, too, if you'd like. We obviously need to do some strategizing." She looked around the room. "*After* the boys have done some cleaning."

"How about me?" asked the Grandfatherly One, sounding testy.

Mom looked startled. "Of course you're welcome to stay, Mr Komquist. I just didn't think you were able to eat."

"Well, I'm not. But it's still nice to be asked."

Mom actually blushed a little. "We'll be delighted to have you. Please let me know if there's anything I can do to make you comfortable."

"Why, thank you, ma'am. Actually, just knowing you'll take Beebo off our hands – so to

speak, since in my case I don't have any hands –
does a great deal to ease my mind."

"Glad to be of service," said Mom. "Now, you
guys get this mess taken care of while I fix supper."

She went into the kitchen. I could hear her
humming as she started to work.

"What," I said, "was *that* all about?"

Beebo smiled. "What you humans call cuteness
does have its useful aspects."

"I'd better call the embassy to let Shhh-foop
know we'll be eating dinner here," said McNally.

"You'll have to use the regular phone system,"
said Pleskit bitterly. "Tim and I no longer have a
direct line."

McNally went into the hall. When he came
back a few minutes later, he was smiling. "Ms
Buttsman was delighted with the news that we
wouldn't be back," he reported. "I think she's
always happier when we're gone."

"Ms Buttsman doesn't know a good thing when
she sees it," said Mom soothingly. "Why don't
you come into the kitchen with me and peel some
potatoes, McNally?"

McNally looked at us and rolled his eyes, then

smiled and followed Mom into the kitchen. I had a sudden panicky moment when I wondered if I had just seen a spark of romance. I stuffed the idea down. It was entirely too weird to think of Mom being interested in someone – though, if I had to pick a father replacement, I must say McNally would be high on my list.

I went to get the dictionary and some telephone books to stack on a chair, so Beebo would have a place to sit.

"That sure smells good," said the Grandfatherly One when supper was on the table and we were all sitting down.

He was on the table, too, stationed at one end like some sort of weird TV set.

"It's just hamburgers," said Mom, blushing a little.

"When you haven't eaten real food for several years, even simple things become greatly appealing," said the Grandfatherly One.

"Some simple things are easier than others," growled McNally, who was thumping the end of the ketchup bottle without any success.

"I can help with that," said Beebo eagerly. Hopping on to the table, he waved his hands at the bottle. It floated out of McNally's grasp. Beebo made some more gestures. The bottle tipped end-up, shook itself a few times, and deposited a big glob of ketchup on McNally's burger.

"Anyone else?" he asked eagerly.

"I could use some," I said, standing up and holding out my plate.

Shake. Shake. Shake. *Splat!* Out came another blob of ketchup.

Mom cleared her throat. We all looked at her. "Beebo, I hope you won't think this is rude," she said. "But on our planet we prefer not to have the guests stand on the table during dinner."

McNally almost snorted hamburger through his nose.

Beebo batted his big eyes at Mom. "*Gleep de reepdeep!*" he exclaimed. "I am *so* sorry! Please forgive my rudeness."

He scrambled back into his seat.

Mom looked at him intensely. "Was that . . . uh . . . magic you were just doing?"

Beebo laughed. "Not magic, Mrs Tompkins.

Just a manipulation of the local gravitational and magnetic fields. It's simple, if you have the right internal organs."

"Oh," said Mom.

After supper we had another long talk, but about the only thing we decided was that Beebo should stay with us until we could figure out a way to contact his people.

"I'll make up a bed for you," said Mom. "I can put it in one of Tim's dresser drawers."

"You don't need to go to all that trouble," said Beebo.

"It's no trouble," replied Mom sharply. "It will be easy, since there's nothing else in them."

All right, so I'm supposed to put away my own clothes after she has washed and folded them.

So sometimes I forget.

Does that make me a bad person?

You would have thought so when we took Beebo into my room.

"*Glasparaznik!*" he cried. "Has some unfortunate and unforeseeable gravitational/magnetic event taken place here?"

"No," said Mom disgustedly. "This is the way it *always* looks."

"Fascinating," said Beebo. "On my planet you could be executed for this."

"If that was a joke, it rates a two," I said. "At best."

"Depends on your sense of humour," replied Beebo with a smile.

Getting ready for bed was interesting. Beebo climbed back into the broken bodysuit and retrieved several items, including a weird-looking pair of alien pyjamas and a tiny book.

"What's that?" I asked, when he started writing in it.

"My diary. Do you want to see it?"

I was a little surprised that he would show me his diary, until I was actually holding it in my hands and realized, of course, that I could not read a word he had written.

Even so, the little book was kind of interesting. The pages were tissue-thin yet incredibly tough. But they weren't see-through like tissue. I wondered what they were made of.

"The diary is part of my class assignment," said Beebo, as I handed it back to him.

It seemed kind of gallant, in a weird way, that he was continuing to work on his assignment even while he was stranded here.

As I climbed into bed that night, I was feeling pretty good. Another alien on the planet, and he was staying in my dresser. This was definitely a cool thing. Then, just as I was drifting off to sleep, Beebo said softly, "Tim, please take me to school with you on Monday."

I sat up. "You've got to be kidding!"

"No. I'm afraid to stay alone."

"What are you afraid of?"

"I don't know," he said uneasily. "My people just don't like being alone."

I didn't like the idea. But Beebo climbed out of my dresser and scrambled up on to my bed. Sitting on my chest, he stared at me with those big eyes of his and said, "Please, oh please, please, please, Tim." He clasped his hands together and continued to beg. "Please, please, please. I will be seized with terror if I am forced to stay here alone all day. Please take me with you. I will be good. I will be quiet. I will not cause any trouble. *Just don't leave me alone!*"

I consider myself a master of begging, but Beebo's performance was impressive even by my standards. I could feel myself weakening.

"But you're supposed to stay a secret," I said. "So how can I take you to school?"

Beebo thought for a second. "Put me in your backpack!" he cried, as if he had just thought of the most brilliant idea in the world.

"You can't stay in my backpack all day!"

"It's better than being here alone," said Beebo, tears welling up in his huge eyes.

I sighed. "All right, I'll take you to school with me."

Dumber words were never spoken.

10

MORAL DILEMMA

Tim called the embassy on Saturday morning. He didn't call on the comm-device, of course, since that had been taken away from me. He called on the regular phone, which meant I could not see or smell him as we talked. I found this highly annoying. Communication is hard enough without having some of the basic clues taken away.

"What is up, fellow star traveller?" I asked.

"Well, uh, Beebo's got a request. He wants to come to school with us on Monday."

"That's a terrible idea!" I cried. "Tell him he can't do it."

"Well, uh, I sort of already told him it was all right."

I tried not to let my *sphen-gnut-ksher* emit a bolt of energy that would fry the phone's circuits. Lowering my voice, I said intensely, "Tim, have you gone *crazy*?"

"Aw, you should have seen the little guy, Pleskit. He was so terrified of being left alone, I just couldn't say no. He promised not to cause any trouble. I told him he could stay in my backpack."

I farted the small and fragrant fart of understanding. This, of course, did not communicate anything to Tim, partly because with the inferior technology we were using the smell was not transmitted, partly because Earthlings can barely interpret smell anyway. (For me, coming to this planet has been a little like moving to a world where no one can hear would be for most Earthlings.)

As for my understanding of Beebo's fears, that came naturally enough from the fact that Tim and I had been stranded on an alien planet ourselves. I knew from personal experience that terror can overwhelm a being caught in such a situation.

That still did not mean I thought taking Beebo to school was a good idea – or even a possible one.

"Have you forgotten the security devices?" I asked. "We couldn't get him into the building even if we wanted to."

"That's why I'm calling you. I figured you could work out some way to get the little guy past the scanners."

Resisting my urge to scream, I said, "Don't you think I have enough problems with the Fatherly One as it is?" I took a deep breath. "Even if we could get Beebo into school, do you really think he can keep from letting people know he's there?"

"He's promised," said Tim.

I didn't say anything, but I wasn't sure what a promise from Beebo was worth.

"Don't forget," persisted Tim, "Beebo has at

least as much reason to want to keep himself a secret as we do."

I thought about that. "True enough. All right, I'll see what I can do."

Tim turned away from the phone to repeat my words to Beebo.

In the background I heard a little voice squeak, "*Ipsky pekoobies!* Thank you, Pleskit!"

It was such a delightfully happy sound that I almost forgot what a bad idea this was probably going to be.

No sooner had I finished talking to Tim than the dreaded Ms Buttsman loomed up behind me. "Your Fatherly One wishes to speak to you, Pleskit," she said, sounding happier than I like to hear her. It's not that I don't want Ms Buttsman to be happy. It's just that she seems to take great pleasure in my misery or discomfort.

My *sphen-gnut-ksher* emitted a guilty odour. I could tell from the twitching of Ms Buttsman's nose that she detected the fruity aroma. Fortunately, she was not capable of understanding what it meant.

In the days since Tim and I returned from our adventure in space, I had seen the Fatherly One far more frequently than I was used to. Alas, while that is something I had long desired, our meetings were not usually about pleasant matters.

This one was no exception.

"Pleskit, I need to make you aware of some things," said the Fatherly One when I entered his office.

I would have been happier if he had bothered to say hello first. Then I saw the degree of concern on his face and decided not to be upset about the lack of greeting.

"What is troubling you, O Fatherly One?"

"I have two things on my mind. Number one: the Galactic Inspection Team is arriving on Monday."

I felt my *clinkus* tighten. This would not be a good time for Beebo to act up.

"I hardly need to stress that we must make a good impression on them," said my Parental Unit. "Though there is residual goodwill for you across the galaxy for the part you played in thwarting Mikta-makta-mookta's plan to destroy the first Grand *Urpelli*, there is also great resentment of our family because the second Grand *Urpelli* was included with the Earth franchise." He paused, then said, "The second item I want to speak about is more troubling."

I barely managed to keep from blurting out, "What could be more troubling than *that*?" – which would have been a big mistake, since I should have found news of the team's arrival merely interesting, not the terror-inducing statement that it actually was.

The Fatherly One paused for some time before speaking. "My second concern is very private."

I wondered, briefly, if he had become involved in some romantic entanglement. Then, for a horrible moment, I wondered if he had somehow found out about Beebo. "Are you sure this is something I should know about?" I asked cautiously.

"Yes. And you are the *only* one I am telling, for I do not know who else to trust." He paused and gestured for me to step closer to him. I joined him in the command pod. At a signal from the Fatherly One, the pod closed. We were now completely shielded from anyone hearing us, either directly or with any kind of electronic equipment.

"What is troubling you, O Fatherly One?" I asked, more nervous than ever.

11

THE BACKPACK

The Fatherly One paused a long time before speaking. When he finally did begin, I understood why he was so troubled. Looking at his hands, he said, "I fear we have another traitor on the embassy staff. Too much information has been leaking out. Most of it is not highly confidential, but people are far too aware of my comings and goings. I am concerned that someone is giving out this information. Or selling it."

"Do you have any idea who it is?" I asked, feeling a little sick at the idea. Even the dreadful Ms Buttsman did not strike me as the sort to be a traitor.

The Fatherly One tweaked his *sphen-gnut-ksher*. "No. I am *smorgle*-broken by the very thought of it. It was bad enough with Mikta-matka-mookta. I do not think I can stand it again."

I understood. Loyalty and honour are important concepts for us on Hevi-Hevi.

Of course, that makes it especially disturbing when loyalty and honour seem to be at war with each other – as, for example, in the current situation, where loyalty to the Fatherly One would prompt me to turn my back on Beebo (or even turn him in to the Inspection Team), yet honour seemed to say this was not the right thing to do.

"Anyway," said the Fatherly One, "I cannot share this fear with anyone else, for I am not sure who to trust. I just wanted to ask you to keep your nose open and be extra careful."

I left the office of my Parental Unit feeling great uneasiness about the danger of a traitor on staff and more uncertain than ever about what I should do regarding Beebo.

Fortunately – for Beebo, at least – as I was passing the chambers of *Wakkam* Akkim, I heard her performing a complex chant. Her voice was weirdly beautiful, and from the first snatch of words I could tell this was something I needed to hear. So I sat down outside her door to listen for a while. The chant turned out to be a kind of prayer or invocation, requesting strength to do what you think is right, no matter what the circumstances.

When she was done, I sighed and got to my feet.

Then I spent most of the weekend trying to devise a method of keeping the school's scanners from detecting Beebo as we brought him into the building.

I finished the shielding device for Tim's backpack late on Sunday afternoon. An hour or so later

McNally and I asked Ralph-the-driver to take us to Tim's apartment, so I could install the shielding in Tim's backpack. (We didn't explain why we were going to Ralph, of course. I loved the fact that he never asked questions.)

"I'm glad you're here," said Tim when we arrived. "Beebo's been wearing me out. Half the time he's telling me jokes that have me laughing so hard I can't stand up – at least, the ones that I can understand do. Alien humour can be very weird."

"It's not weird, it's profound," said Beebo, who was sitting on the couch with a comic book floating in front of him. A page turned without him touching it.

Tim rolled his eyes. "The rest of the time he's offering to help me clean my room!"

"It's a matter of health and safety," said Beebo.

"Isn't he adorable?" said Mrs Tompkins.

Tim rolled his eyes again.

"Well, I've got the shield," I said. "Where's your backpack?"

"Just a second. I'll have to empty it out."

Watching Tim empty his backpack was like

seeing the laws of physics violated. It was hard to believe so much stuff had been held in such a small space.

"So that's what happened to that potholder!" said his mother, snatching a piece of fabric from the pile growing at Tim's feet. "What's it doing in here?"

"I used it for padding when I had to take that egg to school," said Tim.

"That was three months ago!" said his mother sharply, as she bent to retrieve another item from the pile. By the time he was done, she had accumulated a small stack of household goods that had found their way into Tim's backpack and not been seen again until this moment, including a screwdriver, three spoons, the remote control for the TV set, a tube of lipstick ("I was going to use it for art class," he explained), and a flowerpot.

He also removed several truly dismaying food items, some of which seemed to have sprouted life-forms of their own.

"Do you think I will be safe in there?" asked Beebo nervously.

"I'll disinfect it for you," said Mrs Tompkins,

taking the pack and giving Tim a look that might have caused a weaker person to crumble into dust on the spot. Then she brought some milk and cookies – Mrs Tompkins makes very good cookies, and they are something I am going to suggest to the Fatherly One that we consider for export to other planets – and we had a snack while she went to clean the backpack. After a few minutes McNally went out to help her. I could tell that Tim wanted to go check up on them but did not dare.

While they were gone I motioned for Tim to come close to me.

"Take this," I said quietly, handing him a small device.

"What is it?"

"A portable comm-device. I really shouldn't be giving it to you, but until this crisis with Beebo is over, I think we need a way to make direct contact despite the Fatherly One's disapproval."

"Good idea," said Tim.

I had just finished showing him how to use the device when Mrs Tompkins returned with the backpack.

"Here you go, Beebo," she said cheerfully. "Fresh as a daisy!" She turned her attention to Tim, and her smile faded. "And it wasn't easy, I want to tell you. We're going to have to have another little talk about this kind of thing, bub."

Tim sighed.

I took the backpack from Mrs Tompkins and installed the shield I had created. "Here," I said, when I had finished. "Try it on for size."

Beebo climbed into the pack. It was a perfect fit.

"Oh, thank you, thank you, thank you, Pleskit," he said happily. "You'll be really glad you helped me. I won't be any trouble. You'll see."

12

BEEBO AGAINST THE DARK SIDE

On Monday morning I helped Beebo get settled in the backpack, then hopped on my bike and rode to school.

Jordan must have taken one of his obnoxious pills before he came to school that day, because his rottenness was in full bloom. "Hey, look!" he said, when Pleskit and I walked into the room. "It's Pleskit and that other kid – the one from outer space."

For a horrifying moment I thought he knew I had Beebo in my backpack. Then I realized he was talking about *me*.

In case I had any doubts, Jordan immediately clarified his statement. "Yeah, monster maker, I'm talking 'bout you. I've been taking a poll. Turns out only ten per cent of the people in our class think you were actually born on this planet."

Brad Kent snorted in approval. "Good one," he said, slapping Jordan on the back.

I could feel myself start to blush. "If you guys are typical Earthlings, I'd rather be an alien anyway," I said.

Jordan scowled, but before he could do anything, Ms Weintraub ordered us all to our seats.

I carefully hung the backpack with Beebo in it on the back of my chair. "You okay in there?" I whispered, bending close to the top as I adjusted one of the straps.

"*Oksey-dokery!*" said Beebo happily. "By the way, your classmate is disgusting. His humour is extremely low-grade."

I sat down.

The first part of the morning was pretty quiet. It wasn't until a little after ten o'clock that Jordan made his first wisecrack at my expense.

No sooner had the words left his mouth than his pencil rolled off his desk.

When he bent to get it, it rolled away from his fingers.

With a growl, he snatched it up.

I should have figured it out then, of course. But I was daydreaming about Linnsy . . . Linnsy *vec* Bur . . . and wondering where they were. So it wasn't until the third time Jordan's pencil hit the floor and I heard Ms Weintraub snap, "Jordan, will you stop fooling around?" that I realized Beebo must be causing it to happen.

I let out a little snort of laughter.

"Something funny, Tim?" asked Ms Weintraub sharply.

"Sorry," I said quickly. "Just a little gas."

Several of the guys laughed, and Chris Mellblom gave me the thumbs-up sign. Most of the girls, on the other hand, rolled their eyes as if they thought I was too crude to live.

Funny as Beebo's prank was – and I was certainly glad to see Jordan getting frustrated and embarrassed – the situation did nothing to improve my own life, since Jordan was pretty sure Pleskit and I had something to do with it.

The thing was, whenever Jordan was steamed at either of us, I was the one he took it out on, since I don't have a personal bodyguard like Pleskit does – not to mention a *sphen-gnut-ksher* that can zap anyone who tries to hassle me too much. So I knew there was trouble coming.

About halfway through the morning I felt something jab me in the shoulder. After a minute I realized it was Beebo's finger poking me through the material of the backpack. At first I thought he was just trying to be annoying. But after he had poked me several times I got up and opened the pack, as if I was getting out a book or something.

Beebo was sitting in the bottom of the pack. He had his legs crossed, and he looked very unhappy.

"I gotta pee!" he whispered.

Yikes! Why hadn't we thought of that earlier? Of course, with alien biology, who could tell if they even needed to pee? For all I knew, Beebo had a metabolism that would let him get through a whole day without having to go to the bathroom. Heck, for all I knew, he didn't pee at all.

Except that now I knew he did.

But now what? Even if I got permission to go to the boys' room, I couldn't just pick up my backpack and head out the door. Ms Weintraub would be sure I was up to something.

I bent closer to the opening of the pack and put my hand in, as if I were trying to find something. "You'll just have to wait!" I hissed.

Beebo's big eyes got even bigger. He didn't say a thing, just nodded and squeezed his legs together. He looked so pathetic it nearly killed me.

I sat down, trying to figure out how to get Beebo out of the room.

A minute later Ms Weintraub came down the aisle, checking on people's work.

Beebo whimpered as she walked past.

Ms Weintraub gave me a funny look. "Was that you, Tim?"

"Sorry," I said. "My sneaker squeaked on the floor."

I noticed Rafaella staring at me suspiciously.

"Oh, geez," I said quickly. "I just remembered! My mother asked me to give something to McNally. I'd better take it to him before I forget. You know how I am."

Ms Weintraub nodded. "Indeed I do," she said. But she had a funny look on her face, and suddenly I wondered if I had made a mistake by saying my mother had sent something to McNally. But I didn't have time to worry about it. I bolted out of my chair, grabbed the backpack, and scurried to the back of the room. "There's something in here for you," I said, speaking quietly.

McNally knew what was in my backpack, of course, though he couldn't say anything. But I could tell from the way he rolled his eyes that I was going to pay for this sooner or later.

I went back to my seat. I saw McNally peek into the backpack. A few minutes later he went to speak to Ms Weintraub. Then he slipped out of the room, taking the backpack with him. He came back a few minutes later, still carrying the pack, and when I looked at him he nodded. So, that was one problem solved.

Now all I had to worry about was Jordan.

It didn't take long for him to make his move. When the class went outside for a break later that morning, I retrieved the pack from McNally. Pleskit and I had gone to the spot we like to hang out when Jordan came storming up and said, "All right, what's going on, Tompkins? I know you and Pleskit Purplepants were making that stuff fall off my desk."

"We had nothing to do with it," said Pleskit sincerely.

"Come on, think about it, Jordan," I said. "Has Pleskit ever demonstrated telekinetic powers?"

That slowed him down just a little.

"So there's no reason to think he's doing it now," I said. "No reason to think anything other than that you're having a sudden burst of clumsiness."

"You're pressing your luck, monster maker," said Jordan. He glanced at McNally, who was standing near-by. I didn't have to look myself to know that he would be pretending to ignore us while he was, in reality, watching like a hawk.

Jordan's lip curled into a truly masterful sneer. "You won't always have that big lunk behind you, you know," he said, just softly enough so that McNally couldn't hear.

He turned to walk away.

As he did, Beebo struck again.

13

THE WITNESS

Jordan happened to be wearing baggy trousers that day. So when all the buttons popped off the front, it wasn't surprising that they dropped down to his knees.

He stumbled and fell.

The sight of Jordan lying flat on his face with his trousers halfway down his legs and his plaid boxer shorts in full view filled me with a weird combination of amusement and terror. There was no way he could blame the event on me and Pleskit. Even so, it was a dead cinch he would be convinced it had been our fault.

Which, in a way, it was.

It didn't help that most of the rest of the sixth grade experienced only the amusement. The gales of laughter that greeted Jordan's detrousering were only going to feed his fury.

Jordan does *not* like to be laughed at.

"Beebo!" I hissed over my shoulder. "Don't do anything like that again!"

"Just trying to help," replied his tiny voice, sounding hurt.

"You'll help me get killed!" I said.

I spent the afternoon in a state of terror, wondering how my enemy would try to get his revenge. The worst part of it was that, even though Pleskit offered to give me a ride home, I still had to stay after school to work with Ms Weintraub.

"I would come back and get you if I could," said Pleskit miserably. "But the Galactic Inspection Team is arriving today, and the Fatherly One insists that I be present."

"I understand," I said gloomily. "Just make sure you can come to my funeral."

The after-school session seemed to last forever, mostly because I had a hard time focusing on how to multiply decimals while simultaneously worrying about how soon I was going to die.

When Ms Weintraub finally gave up and let me go, I hurried into the hall, looked around to make sure no one was near-by, then opened the backpack.

"You okay in there?" I asked.

"I gotta pee again," said Beebo miserably. "I think my eyeballs are starting to float."

I sighed and took him into the boys' room. He went into one of the stalls. A few minutes later I heard a flush. The door opened, and he strolled back out – an odd sight, since he was barely as tall as the toilet.

"*Feezle dee-goopus!*" he said. "I feel better."

"Yeah, well, I'm afraid I'm not going to feel so good pretty soon."

"Why not?" asked Beebo, looking so genuinely concerned I almost forgot that he was the one who got me into this trouble.

"Because Jordan's gonna kill me for what you did to him in the playground today."

Beebo looked shocked. "They warned me that this was a savage and terrible world, but I did not think it was *that* dangerous!"

"I don't mean he's really going to kill me – though I might wish he had by the time he's done with me. I don't know *what* he's gonna do, actually. Most of the time he just hassles me by teasing me. But he was so mad this time, I think he's probably gonna punch my lights out."

"What lights?" asked Beebo.

"It's just an expression. It means he's going to beat me up."

"Well, it may not be murder, but I still find that shockingly violent," said Beebo.

"You must not have studied our world that much," I muttered.

"I'm here to study humour, not tragedy."

I sighed. "Just get in the backpack," I said.

I left the school through the back door. I was

looking from side to side, checking for any sign of Jordan.

My caution didn't do me any good. As I walked past the Dumpster, he stepped out from behind it and said, "All right, Tompkins. What's the deal?"

"Yeah," said Brad, who was, not surprisingly, right there beside him. "What's the deal?"

"No deal," I said. I held out my hands. "See? I don't even have a deck of cards."

"Ha very ha," said Jordan, stepping toward me.

Brad had gone a little to my left and was approaching from that side. I felt like an elk that's been cut out of the herd by a pack of wolves.

Jordan's fists were clenching. "Talk, Tompkins," he said, stepping even closer.

"Yeah," said Brad. "Talk!"

I wondered if I should slip out of the backpack. Odds were good the three of us were going to be rolling on the ground soon, with me mostly on the bottom, and I didn't want to squash Beebo. On the other hand, if I did take off the pack, the very action might draw attention to it, make Jordan wonder what was inside . . .

I was dying to say, "Beebo, if you've got any

tricks in mind, now's the time to use them!" Except that would have made it clear what was going on. Besides, detrousering Jordan again at this point would do nothing but prove I had had something to do with it the first time. And I knew Beebo's powers weren't strong enough to lift Jordan and Brad and drop them in the Dumpster.

I swallowed hard.

Jordan and Brad moved closer, making a slow circle around me. Then Jordan stopped right in front of me. He reached out to grab me. I hadn't been this scared since we were attacked by those terrible pod creatures on Billa Kindikan.

"Time for us to have a little talk, Tim," said Jordan.

He grabbed the front of my shirt. His right hand balled into a fist.

Then, to my astonishment, Rafaella stepped out from the far side of the Dumpster.

She was holding a camera.

"Well, well, well," she said, her voice deadly serious. "What a perfect photo op." She lifted the camera and looked through the eyepiece. "Everybody smile!"

"Get out of here, Rafaella," said Jordan. "This is none of your business."

She pressed the shutter button, and the camera clicked. "You'll look better if you smile, Jordan," she said grimly. "Of course, this probably isn't a good time to do anything you might not want people to know about. Pictures do have a way of getting around."

Then she smiled at him.

A long moment passed while the four of us – Jordan, Brad, me, and Rafaella – stood as if frozen.

Finally Jordan looked at Brad and made a get-out-of-here gesture with his head. Brad started to back away.

"This isn't over, Tompkins," said Jordan. "You either, Rafaella." Then he turned and stalked away.

Maybe it wasn't over, but the crisis was past for the moment. I felt my knees wobble, and it was all I could do to keep from falling down.

I turned to Rafaella. "Thanks," I said.

She shrugged.

"How did you happen to be here?" I asked.

She shook her head. "I didn't just *happen* to be here, Tim. After what went on outside today, I knew Jordan would be planning to hassle you after school."

I looked at her carefully. "So why did you decide to do something about it?"

She turned off her camera and put it in her own backpack. "My father has a saying he likes to quote. He says that all that is necessary for evil to triumph is for good people to remain silent." She gestured in the direction Jordan and Brad had disappeared. "I guess I just couldn't stay silent any longer."

"You're the first person who's ever helped me with Jordan," I said.

She shrugged. "Today was worse than usual. Besides, it's the first time I figured out something to do."

I smiled. "I owe you a favour."

"Good. You can repay it right now."

"How?" I asked, suddenly feeling nervous.

"Tell me what's in your backpack."

I was trying to decide whether I could lie to someone who had just saved my life when Beebo coughed.

It was just a tiny cough.

But it was unquestionably a cough.

Equally unquestionably, it was coming from my backpack.

Rafaella looked at me and raised an eyebrow.

I sighed. "Promise you won't tell?"

She nodded solemnly, then put a finger on her lips. "Consider me sworn to silence."

I shrugged out of the shoulder straps and pulled the backpack around in front of me. "Come here," I said.

She walked over to join me.

I undid the buckle and lifted the top of my backpack.

Rafaella peered in, then cried out in horror.

14

THE INSPECTION TEAM

I could not stop fretting about Tim as McNally and I travelled back to the embassy after school that day. However, once we reached the embassy, I had to turn my attention to my own problem – the Inspection Team from the Interplanetary Trading Federation.

"They're hee-e-e-e-re!" sang Shhh-foop, as McNally and I entered the embassy kitchen. At first I thought she was referring to the two of us. But she was sliding frantically about the floor, her tentacles twirling around her head, and after a moment I realized she meant that the Inspection Team had arrived. I could tell she was in the midst of preparing some grand meal for them.

"Don't worry about us, Shhh-foop," I said. "I can get a snack for myself."

"But I will not have time to make coffee for the weary Just McNally," she warbled fretfully.

McNally doesn't really like to have the "Mr" attached to his name. Therefore, whenever he meets someone new he says, "It's McNally. Just . . . McNally." This has had the side effect of convincing Shhh-foop that the proper way to address him is as "Just McNally". He seems to find this amusing, and it probably makes up for the fact that the Fatherly One and Ms Buttsman *always* call him *Mr* McNally.

"Don't worry about the coffee, Shhh-foop," said McNally now, working hard to sound regretful. "I'll manage somehow."

* * *

We had been back for only a few moments when the speaker above the kitchen door belched for attention and informed me that I was wanted in the office of the Fatherly One.

"Time to meet the Inspection Team," I said.

"Good luck, champ," said McNally.

Beezle Whompis and Ms Buttsman were both waiting outside the Fatherly One's office.

"Don't worry, Pleskit," said Beezle Whompis. "You'll do fine."

At the same time, Ms Buttsman was fussing over me, straightening my collar, brushing dust that only she could see off my sleeve, and generally acting in a way almost guaranteed to make a being worry.

The two of them were like matter and antimatter. Sometimes I wondered if they would explode if they got too close together.

Right now I wondered if either of them was the traitor.

When I entered the office of the Fatherly One, I saw that the team consisted of three members.

The Fatherly One stood to introduce me.

"Gentlebeings," he said, speaking in Standard Galactic. "I would like you to meet my childling, Pleskit Meenom."

"Ah, the hero of the galaxy," said one of the team, a short, stocky being. I was a little embarrassed when they all began to applaud, each in *yeeble*'s own way – which ranged from slapping hands against knees to a very loud tongue-clucking sound.

The Fatherly One took me to each of them in turn. The first was named Earla <bzzz> Fif!, or Fif! for short. Fif! was tall and had stiff, transparent wings growing from her shoulders. The wings reached nearly to the floor. Their edges looked sharp, and though I couldn't be sure without asking an impolite question, I had a feeling they were probably as useful for weapons as they were for flying.

"And this is Sookutan Krimble," said the Fatherly One, guiding me to the next member of the team. *Frek* Krimble (*Frek* is the proper term of address for certain important beings from *yeeble*'s planet) was also tall. *Yeeble*'s orange skin and scales reminded me of Beebo, but the stylish

black robe and the dignified way *yeeble* carried *yeeble*self could not have been more different from our cute but mischievous visitor.

The third member of the team was a short, blue being with enormous eyes and a three-pronged nose who was called Paznod 5. "Actually," she said with a musical laugh, "my full name is Paznod [three-tone whistle] Five. But I only use that for very formal occasions. Let me tell you again, Pleskit, how impressed I am with what you and your friends accomplished on Billa Kindikan. We are in your debt." She lowered her eyes, then added, "If it were up to me, we would not bother with this inspection at all. It seems ungracious. But the uproar occasioned by the discovery of a Grand *Urpelli* in your Fatherly One's territory makes it necessary."

"I understand," I said, nodding my head and farting respectfully.

The diplomats began talking to the Fatherly One again. They droned on, and though I was trying to be polite and look interested, I was having a hard time staying awake – until I felt the portable communicator I had given to Tim start vibrating in my pocket.

Without intending to, I leaped to my feet.

"Are you all right, Pleskit?" asked the Fatherly One, scowling slightly.

"I'm fine," I said quickly, sticking my hand in my pocket to try to cover the device so that no one would see it vibrating. "It's just that I suddenly remembered something important I need to take care of regarding school."

"I'm sure the boy has better things to do than listen to us talk," said Fif!. "Why don't you let him go, Meenom?"

The Fatherly One's face tightened, and he looked a little suspicious. But he bent his *sphengnut-ksher* in acceptance. "We'll see you for dinner, Pleskit," he said. "Formal garb tonight, please."

"I look forward to it with pleasure," I said, relieved that my brain was still working well enough to respond with the diplomatically proper words.

I bid each of the visitors goodbye, then hurried to my room.

I was very worried. I knew Tim would not be

using the comm-device unless it was an emergency. I feared he had been attacked by Jordan and was calling for help.

When I was finally alone I pulled the device from my pocket and pushed the Connect button.

"Tim. Tim, are you there?"

I was relieved to hear his voice. The relief lasted only an instant – just long enough for me to hear what he was saying.

"Pleskit, we need help. Beebo is sick."

"How sick?"

"I can't tell. It looks serious." Tim paused, then said, "I think he may be dying!"

15

THE DAYLIGHT RIDE OF EARGON FOOZ

I felt the dim haziness of *kleptra* stealing over me. It would have been pleasant to succumb to its dark emptiness, to just let go of the world and all its problems. But I could not do that. Beebo's life might be at stake.

But what should I do?

I had to go get him, that was clear. No Earth

doctor would have the slightest idea what to do for him.

Could I do that without alerting the Inspection Team to what was going on?

"Pleskit?" said Tim, sounding worried. "Pleskit, are you still there?"

"Yes, I'm here. I'm just thinking. Where are you?"

"We're in back of the school, at the door farthest from the parking lot, the one near the art room."

"All right, don't move. I'll figure out some way to come and get you."

"What about your Fatherly One?" asked Tim, sounding worried.

"I don't know!" I snapped. "I'll worry about that next. Don't go anywhere."

"Don't worry," said Tim, sounding scared. "We won't."

"Hurry, Pleskit," said another, familiar voice.

"Rafaella?" I asked in surprise. "What are you doing there?"

"Never mind that now," said Tim. "Just get over here!"

"Right. See you soon."

I clicked off the pocket communicator and closed my eyes to think. I decided the best thing to do was go for McNally.

To my despair, when I went to the kitchen to look for him, Shhh-foop told me he had been called in to meet the Inspection Team.

Now what? Even if I could have gotten Beebo into the embassy without alerting anyone to what was going on, there was no way I could get McNally *out* of that meeting without causing a scene and creating questions.

And without McNally, how could I get over to the school?

Then it hit me! Eargon Fooz! She was the only adult being in the embassy not tied up with the fuss created by the arrival of the Inspection Team. And it didn't matter that she couldn't drive – she could *run* to the school, maybe even get there faster than the limo would have, since she wouldn't be stopping for traffic lights and so on.

I raced to her living quarters, which were on one of the upper floors, as she preferred to be somewhat solitary. I burped a command to her door. It took my picture and showed it to her inside, indicating that I was requesting admission.

A second later the door slid open.

She had been decorating her room to look like her home on Billa Kindikan. One wall had a three-dimensional jungle mural. Pictures of her five children were mounted on a pole in the centre of the room.

She extended her humanlike arms in greeting. "What can I do for you, Pleskit?"

"I have a friend who's in trouble. Can you take me to him, help me bring him back here?"

I was not surprised when she agreed without even asking any more questions. That's the kind of being she is.

We took the transport tube down to the garage. Without even trying to explain to the astonished Ralph-the-driver what was going on, we galloped up the ramp and out through Thorncraft Park. Soon we were pounding our way through the streets of Syracuse, Eargon Fooz's powerful legs beating out a rhythm on the concrete pavements as we headed for the school. It was a quiet weekday afternoon, and most people were still at work. A few pedestrians gawked or cried out or cheered as we went rattling by. Some tried to chase us, but they couldn't keep up, of course. Fortunately, no one was near when we came galloping into the school's parking lot – not more than ten minutes after we left the embassy.

"They're around back," I said to Eargon Fooz, who was barely panting despite her exertions.

We found Tim and Rafaella near the back door of the school. They were kneeling, and Rafaella was cradling something in her arms.

I slid off Eargon Fooz's back.

"What's going on?" I asked, rushing over to them.

They didn't say anything, just pulled back so I could see what they had between them.

Curled in Rafaella's arms was Beebo. He had his knees clutched to his chest, and his skin had faded from its usual bright orange to a pale yellow.

I reached out to touch him.

He felt cold.

At my touch he twitched slightly, then opened

his eyes. "Pleskit?" he asked, reaching one tiny hand toward me. He hadn't moved it more than a few inches before he gave a tiny cough. His arm fell limp, and he closed his eyes again.

16

TOUGH DECISION

I was incredibly relieved when Pleskit showed up
with Eargon Fooz. I had been terrified that Beebo
was going to die before we could get help for him.
I was still terrified when they got there, but it felt
good to have someone show up who ought to
know more about alien biology than we did.

"How did this happen?" asked Pleskit.

I shook my head. "I don't know. We heard him

cough, and when I opened the backpack we found him like this."

Big tears welled up in Rafaella's eyes. "He's so adorable, it's just heartbreaking to see him like that. Can you tell what's the matter with him, Pleskit?"

Pleskit looked really nervous. "It's hard to say," he muttered. "Could be anything from not getting enough air in the backpack to having an allergic reaction to the planet."

Eargon Fooz uttered a weird jumble of sounds.

Pleskit looked distressed as he translated. "She says we have to take him back to the embassy."

"That could end up costing your Fatherly One the Earth franchise!" I cried.

"And your planet its freedom," he replied grimly.

I felt sick. What was the cost of freedom? I knew people fought and died for it. But could you buy it with an innocent life?

I looked down at Beebo. *What is one person worth?* I wondered. It always seemed like a weird question to me. I hear politicians and ministers and talking heads on TV babbling on about how every human life is priceless. They'll pass some law and say, "This is going to cost a million dollars, but if it saves just one life, it's worth it." So does that mean a life is worth a million dollars? And if it's worth a million dollars to save just one life, then how come we let people starve to death when it would cost only a few hundred to feed them for an entire year?

So, what is a life worth?

A fortune?

A planet?

Are some lives worth more than others?

If so, who gets to choose?

My head was starting to spin.

Then Beebo coughed again.

This was just one life, but it was here in our hands. If we didn't do something, that life might end. Yet, if we did the only thing we could, the consequences might be terrible.

Maybe someone older, smarter, stronger, tougher would have made another choice. But I didn't have the courage to just sit there and watch Beebo die.

"Eargon Fooz is right," I said. "We have to get him to the embassy."

"I agree," said Pleskit. "Come on, help me get him into the backpack. Eargon Fooz and I will take him back." He looked at me. "Did you ride your bike today?"

"Yeah. I'll follow you over."

"Me, too," said Rafaella.

Pleskit hesitated, then nodded. "See you there."

I helped him on to Eargon Fooz's back, then carefully handed up the backpack with Beebo in it.

As they galloped off, Rafaella and I went to get our bikes. We didn't talk much as we pedalled over to the embassy. I was busy wondering if Pleskit's Fatherly One was going to blame this whole mess on me – and if he did, just exactly what a powerful alien ambassador might do to a puny little Earth kid who had just cost him a chance at the greatest fortune in the history of the galaxy.

I didn't even think about the other part, the part about what might happen if Meenom was removed from the mission and the planet was assigned to some other, less friendly Trader.

I couldn't.

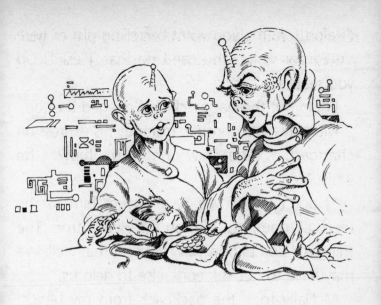

17

THE LAST LAUGH

While Eargon Fooz was carrying us back toward the embassy, I was trying desperately to think of whom I should contact once I got Beebo inside.

I was surprised to find McNally waiting for us at the base of the hook that holds up the embassy. He looked angry, but I was so relieved to see him I didn't care.

"Where have you been?" he demanded.

"Ralph told me you went barrelling out of here on Eargon Fooz. You can't do that, Pleskit! Do you realize—"

I held out the backpack and opened the top.

McNally looked inside. Instantly his expression changed. "What's wrong with him?" he whispered.

"I don't know. We have to get him to the medical room, put him on the Heal-a-tron. The thing is, I don't know how to use it that well. We may have to get someone else to help us."

McNally took the backpack from my hands. "Come on, let's get moving," he said, cradling it gently in his arms. He shook his head. "Man, Pleskit, if we can't keep this under wraps – and right now, I'd say the odds are low – it looks like your father can say goodbye to the biggest stack of money in the galaxy."

"Should we have done something different?" I asked miserably.

McNally didn't say anything, just sort of growled as he shook his head. "What are we gonna do? We can't just let the kid die."

* * *

Once we were inside the embassy we faced the next question – namely, who else to ask for help. The Fatherly One was locked in conference with the Inspection Team. Of course, we could have interrupted by sounding an emergency, but we were still faintly hoping we could handle this in secret – not just for our sake, but for Beebo's.

The Heal-a-tron is fairly easy to use. Unfortunately, it was only set up for the biology of the beings who were actually in the embassy, and I didn't know how to recalibrate it for another species.

"Beezle Whompis is probably our best bet," said McNally. "He's the most apt to be willing to wink at something a little out of line."

But the Fatherly One's secretary had been called into the private conference and was not available.

"Maybe we should call *Wakkam* Akkim," I said. "She can advise us."

To my relief, the *wakkam* was in her room and hurried to join us as soon as we contacted her. She took one look at Beebo and, without even asking where he had come from, said, "Who is best at calibrating the Heal-a-tron?"

"The Fatherly One," I replied.

"Then we shall have to call him immediately. I will fetch him myself. I may be able to do it without alerting the Inspection Team to the fact that we have a . . . situation."

She hurried from the room.

While we were waiting for *Wakkam* Akkim to return with the Fatherly One, I got a call from the guard shack that Tim and Rafaella had arrived. I told the guard to let them in, and in only a few minutes they joined us in the med room.

We stood around the healing table looking at Beebo's pale form. Rarely have I felt so helpless. His body twitched occasionally but otherwise did not move. He barely seemed to be breathing.

Rafaella stood close to Tim, her shoulder almost touching his. She didn't speak, but occasionally reached out as if she wanted to touch Beebo.

I felt the coldness of *pizumpta* creeping over me. What would the Fatherly One say about the trouble I had brought into our home?

What would he say if I cost him the biggest fortune in the galaxy?

And what would it truly mean to the people of Earth if the Fatherly One was removed from his position?

I actually considered hiding behind the door when *Wakkam* Akkim returned with the Fatherly One.

I don't know what I expected him to do. He didn't scream and yell or anything. He just looked sick.

"What has been going on here?" he asked.

Tim came to stand beside me. I appreciated that. I knew he was stepping forward to take his share of the blame.

"Tim and I have been sheltering this being," I said miserably. "He is from a non-Federation planet. I know he does not belong here, but we did not want to turn him in to the Federation because he really hasn't done anything wrong."

"Do you realize what this could cost us?" asked the Fatherly One. "Especially now, with the Inspection Team here?"

His voice was low and cold, as if he could

barely get the words out of his mouth.

Tim and I both nodded miserably.

The Fatherly One looked down at Beebo's tiny body lying on the healing table. He closed his eyes for a moment and shook his head. "All right," he said softly. "I'll deal with you two later. Our first concern must be for the child. Let's see if we can get this thing to work."

He went to the control panel and began to manipulate the dials, buttons, levers, and touch pads. Before long the Heal-a-tron was humming and buzzing. The Fatherly One continued making adjustments, but after a little while he began to mutter to himself. He look puzzled, then distressed, and finally angry.

"The Heal-a-tron says there is nothing wrong with this boy!"

"Nothing that a good laugh couldn't cure!" cried Beebo, sitting up on the table and smiling.

We looked at him in astonishment. His skin had returned to its normal bright orange. His eyes were wide and sparkling. He seemed the picture of health.

"Was this all a joke?" I asked in horror.

Beebo's face got very serious. "Not quite," he said. "Actually, it was more like a test."

With that, he pushed a button on his waistband.

"What did you just do?" asked the Fatherly One.

"I have summoned my mentor," said Beebo. "*Yeeble* is a member of the Inspection Team visiting your embassy and will be here in just a minute."

A sick silence fell over the room.

I couldn't bring myself to look at the Fatherly One. I couldn't stand to think about what we had done to him.

18

FINAL EXAM

When Sookutan Krimble appeared in the doorway of the medical room, I felt sad and weary. Tim and I had tried so hard to do the right thing, tried hard to do it in a way that would not harm anyone, and we had failed. No, worse than failed. We had been betrayed by the very being we were trying to help. It was all I could do to keep from lunging at Beebo and doing something . . . unpleasant.

The Fatherly One would not look at me. I could not tell if it was because he was too angry with me or because he was trying so hard to contain his own emotions.

Frek Krimble stepped into the healing room and gestured for the door to close.

"Well, Meenom," *yeeble* said. "It appears you and your childling are not quite as rigidly upstanding as you like to appear."

Now the Fatherly One did look at me, but I could not read his expression. Then he turned back to Sookutan Krimble and said simply, "We did what we thought was right."

I don't think I have ever been more pleased or proud to be his childling.

Sookutan Krimble smiled. "I was wondering how you would respond to our little test. You are softer than you like to pretend."

The Fatherly One pulled himself up and straightened his shoulders. "So this was all arranged as a trap, is that it? All right, we may as well go tell the others of my failure. I am sure rival Traders all across the galaxy will be celebrating when this news is released."

"You misunderstand me," said *Frek* Krimble, smiling gently. "You did not fail. Quite the opposite. As far as I am concerned, you did exactly the right thing."

"I still do not understand," said the Fatherly One.

Sookutan Krimble put *yeeble*'s hands on the Fatherly One's shoulders. "Not all of us believe that the ferocity of the Federation when it comes to dealing with non-member planets is wise or just. Some of us are working to make the peace that sweeps the stars even sweeter and more widespread. You can think of me as part of the in-house resistance. We are, of necessity, working in secret right now. But there are more of us than you might expect, and we are good friends to have. Before I made my report, I wanted to know what kind of being you are, Meenom – what kind of Trader was in line to control such a fantastic resource as the Grand *Urpelli*. That was why I asked my *kribbl-pam*" – here *yeeble* gestured to Beebo – "to help me conduct a test."

"What's a *kribbl-pam*?" I asked.

"Beebo and I are part of the same family unit," said Sookutan Krimble.

"So your planet is *not* non-Federation!" I said to Beebo accusingly.

"I made that part up," he said, grinning broadly. "But most of the rest of what I said was true. I really do have to make field trips, and study humour, and things like that."

"How can you two be related?" asked Tim, looking back and forth from Beebo to Sookutan Krimble. "You don't even look like you're part of the same species."

This made Beebo laugh uproariously.

"Our biology is at the complicated end of the life scale," said Sookutan Krimble, smiling. "On Frimbat it takes several different life-forms to make a family unit. Beebo and I come from different, yet closely related species." *Yeeble* rolled *yeeble*'s eyes slightly and added, "Obviously, Beebo's species is far sillier than mine. Yet for this reason we value them greatly. They bring considerable joy to our planet."

"Silly is good!" said Beebo, standing on the table and spreading his arms as if he could embrace the entire world. "Laughter is a virtue! And cuteness is a very useful tool for surviving in the world!"

I figured this must be true, since it was probably the only thing that kept me from killing him for what he had put us through.

Sookutan Krimble sighed. "It would actually have been a better test if my *kribbl-pam* were not so infernally cute. But you have to work with what you have available."

Yeeble turned to the Fatherly One. "Deep currents are flowing through the politics of the Trading Federation, and things are more complicated than you may have realized, Meenom. Someday I may come to you for help in our struggle to make things better. For now you have *my* help and my guarantee that you will pass this inspection with flying colours. You also have my admiration for your compassion and wisdom. May the blessings of peace and wealth flow to you, your family, and the planet that is under your protection."

19

TOKENS FROM THE STARS

I can't say I was entirely sorry to see Beebo go. He left separately from Sookutan Krimble, of course, since it would have ruined everything if the rest of the Inspection Team had found out about him. I don't think Meenom really felt at ease until Beebo was off the planet altogether.

He left behind the bodysuit he had been wearing when I first met him. I still have it in my closet. It's a little spooky, since it looks so real.

"What am I going to do with it?" he said, when he asked if I wanted it. "It's not like I can use it to fit in anywhere else."

"I suppose it was never really broken," I said, trying not to sound bitter about the way he had deceived us.

"Actually, it was and still is," said Beebo. "I truly was terrified when that happened, even though I knew my mentor would be arriving soon. Our plan had always been to see if Pleskit and Meenom would offer shelter to an illegal alien. But we didn't know if they would or not, and I was supposed to have my bodysuit for protection if I needed it."

Late that night Mom and I drove the little guy to a spot ten or fifteen miles outside Syracuse where he had stashed his space scooter in an abandoned barn. To keep from being noticed, we put him in an old baby suit of mine that Mom had saved, and strapped him into a car seat we borrowed from our downstairs neighbours.

As we drew close to the spot where he had

stowed the scooter, Beebo said, "I left a small packet of my favourite tricks and puzzles on your dresser for you, Tim. Sort of a thank-you present for helping me. I even made a translation of the instructions. I think you will have fun with them."

"He'll probably blow himself up," said Mom.

"Oh, I don't think so," said Beebo. "Fewer than half of them are potentially lethal."

"Beebo!" cried Mom, putting on the brakes.

Beebo burst out laughing. "Got you, Mrs Tompkins!"

"I'd rate that as a one," growled Mom. "At best." But I could see a smile tugging at *both* corners of her mouth. So I guess it really does pay to be cute.

When we got back to the apartment we found that Beebo had left behind more than his bodysuit and the packet of tricks. (Which looked totally cool, and which I am planning to have a lot of fun with, I can tell you. I'm already trying to figure out some way to give Jordan the "Fizzy Fart Bomb".)

He had also left his diary.

"I guess kids are forgetful all over the galaxy," said Mom when I showed it to her. She sounded half amused, half disgusted.

I took the little book from her hands. "Too bad we can't read it," I said.

When she didn't answer, I glanced up at her. She looked disturbed.

"What's the matter, Mom?"

"Oh, just a thought I had. My father used to say that when people leave something behind, it's because they want an excuse to come back."

"Now, there's a scary idea!"

Mom nodded. "I quite agree. Come on, let's—"

She was interrupted by the doorbell.

"You don't suppose it's Beebo, do you?" I asked nervously.

She took a deep breath. "We'd better go see."

It wasn't. In fact, there was no one there at all. But on the floor, where someone had slid it under the door, was a postcard.

It was a picture of an alien landscape, beautiful but bizarre.

I turned the card over.
The message on the back was simple:

Life is weird. Wish you were here.
Love,
Linnsy vec Bur

20

A LETTER HOME

FROM: Pleskit Meenom, on the occasionally amusing Planet Earth
TO: Maktel Geebrit, on the distant but beloved Planet Hevi-Hevi

Dear Maktel:

I thought you might enjoy seeing these notes that Tim and I made about our latest adventure, especially since you and Tim have become friends, sort of.

Now that the situation is finished, we can laugh about it, and laughter is a very good thing. But we had some pretty tense moments while it was all going on. I have to tell you, sometimes trying to figure out what's right, good, honourable – well, it can can make your brain hurt.

The Fatherly One and I still have a tense matter hanging over us here in the embassy – namely, the question of whether there is a traitor on the staff. I have discussed the matter with the Grandfatherly One, but he has no clues as to who it might be. And I dare not discuss it with anyone else. The Fatherly One has even ordered me not to discuss it with my bodyguard, which is most disturbing.

I will be sure to keep you posted if anything comes up.

The Fatherly One did do something else that was quite amazing: he apologized for getting so wound up in his work that he had been, in a way, twisted out of shape for a time.

"I do not want to lose the Earth franchise," he said. "But neither do I want to lose myself. I regret my threat to remove you from your school, Pleskit, and appreciate that you and Tim were able to see the right thing and do it."

So that was pretty cool (as the Earthlings like to say).

Please give my regards to your Motherly One. I hope you have recovered from our adventures on Billa Kindikan!

Fremmix Bleeblom!

Your pal,

Pleskit

A GLOSSARY OF ALIEN TERMS

Following are definitions for the alien words and phrases appearing for the first time in this book. The number after a definition indicates the chapter where the word first appeared.

Words used by Pleskit are usually of Hevi-Hevian origin. Words and phrases used by Beebo are sometimes Frimbattian, but are mostly Standard Galactic.

For most words we are only giving the spelling. In actual usage, of course, many Hevi-Hevian words would be accompanied by smells and/or body sounds.

Definitions of other extraterrestrial words appearing in this book can be found in the volumes of MY ALIEN CLASSMATE where they were first used. A complete glossary, covering all the extraterrestrial words used in the series, can be found at *www.bruce coville.com*

feezlebort: a herb found in the northern wamp-fields of Hevi-Hevi. *Feezlebort* can be brewed into a fizzy soft drink that has a delicious tangy taste, but paralyses the tongue for about five minutes. For this reason Parental Units often encourage children to develop a taste for the drink, as it sometimes provides the only silence they can get in a day. (2)

feezle dee-goopus: This was originally an expression of relief, uttered in thanks by Parental Units who had just given their children some fizzling *feezlebort* and were experiencing the first silence of the day. Eventually it came to be used in any situation where one experiences sudden relief after a period of intense anxiety. (7)

Frek (plural: Frekki): Term of respect for head of the combined Frimbattian family unit. Since a complete family includes six species and a total of seventeen different genders, being *Frek* can be a dangerous, tense, and emotionally difficult job requiring enormous organizational and diplomatic skills, not to mention great physical stamina. *Frekki* are often hired to run huge multiplanetary trading companies, since they consider the job fairly simple, and a pleasant relief from their home lives. (14)

glasparaznik!: A cry of astonished horror, something like "Yikes!", but considerably stronger in meaning. The exclamation mark is part of the standard spelling. (9)

gleep de reepdeep: An expression of embarrassment used when one makes a social faux pas, such as using the wrong table utensil for your soup or accidentally using the fart of derision when you intended to emit the fart of compassion. (Such speech errors are commonly referred to as "butt blurps".) Standard Galactic. (9)

grindlezark: a hideous beast found in the southern wampfields of Hevi-Hevi. Though the *grindlezark* weighs several tons, it never attacks creatures anywhere near its own size, and is known for the way it likes to stalk small, helpless creatures and terrorize them before it eats them. If the *grindlezark* lived on Earth, its favourite meal would probably be baby bunnies. (2)

ipsky pekoobies: A Frimbattian cry of delight, somewhat similar to "yippee" in meaning. (10)

kribbl-pam: Frimbattian term of relationship,

indicating the third offspring of a mating pair three degrees of specieshood away from either the *Frek* or the *Frek*'s spousal unit. The Frimbattian language has four thousand different terms of relationship, and most of the first two years of school are spent learning them. (18)

paznak (plural: paznakki): Bizarre and dangerous life-form that originated on Peldrim Seven, but has spread through much of the galaxy by stowing away on trading ships. No bigger than a human hand, a *paznak* is often described as "a stomach with legs" and can eat seven to ten times its own body weight in a day. A group of *paznakki* can strip an entire field in a matter of hours. (3)

seekl-fingus: Literally, "someone who trips over a grain of sand". The expression is used, derisively, for anyone who is too worried about small details. (5)

wizzik (plural: wizzikki): *Wizzikki* are small, round, hard-shelled insects. Children on Hevi-Hevi sometimes use dead *wizzikki* as pretend currency when they play "Traders and Pirates" and other money games. (7)

MY ALIEN CLASSMATE 10:
Revolt of the Miniature Mutants

Bruce Coville

The hamsters in Pleskit's classroom are beginning to act a little strange. Not only are they becoming more intelligent as each day passes, but they're also becoming bigger and more belligerent. Could their metamorphosis have anything to do with the alien vitamin supplements Pleskit has been giving them? Or is there something more sinister going on . . . ?

MY ALIEN CLASSMATE 11:
There's an Alien in my Underwear

Bruce Coville

Beebo the little alien is back in town, and he's already causing trouble! First, Tim finds his underwear flying from the school flagpole, then Plesket's bodyguard is accidentally locked into another dimension. Is there a more sinister purpose to Beebo's mischief-making? Tim's beginning to suspect so . . .

ALIENS ATE MY HOMEWORK

Bruce Coville

Do you have problems telling lies?
Can you only speak the truth – no matter
how silly? Then you'll know how Rod felt
when his teacher asked about his science
project – because he could only tell her
the truth: 'Aliens ate my homework, Miss
Maloney!'

Of course, nobody believes Rod, so
nobody bothers to ask where the aliens
come from. Just as well – because Rod is
helping Madame Pong and the crazy crew
of the Ferkel on a *very* secret mission . . .

ORDER FORM
Bruce Coville
My Alien Classmate series

0 340 73634 8	There's an Alien in my Classroom!	£3.99
0 340 73635 6	The Attack of the Two-inch Teacher	£3.99
0 340 73636 4	I Lost My Grandfather's Brain	£3.99
0 340 73637 2	Alien Kiss Chase	£3.99
0 340 73638 0	The Science Project of Doom	£3.99
0 340 73639 9	Don't Fry my Veeblex!	£3.99
0 340 73640 2	Too Many Aliens!	£3.99
0 340 73641 0	Snatched From Earth!	£3.99

Rod Allbright Alien series

0 340 65115 6	Aliens Ate My Homework	£3.99
0 340 65116 4	I Left My Sneakers in Dimension X	£3.99
0 340 65355 8	Aliens Stole My Dad	£3.99
0 340 71022 5	Aliens Stole My Body	£3.99

All Hodder Children's books are available at your local bookshop, or can be ordered direct from the publisher. Just tick the titles you would like and complete the details below. Prices and availability are subject to change without prior notice.

Please enclose a cheque or postal order made payable to *Bookpoint Ltd*, and send to: Hodder Children's Books, 39 Milton Park, Abingdon, OXON OX14 4TD, UK.
Email Address: orders@bookpoint.co.uk

If you would prefer to pay by credit card, our call centre team would be delighted to take your order by telephone. Our direct line *01235 400414* (lines open 9.00 am–6.00 pm Monday to Saturday, 24 hour message answering service). Alternatively you can send a fax on *01235 400454*.

TITLE	FIRST NAME		SURNAME	
ADDRESS				
DAYTIME TEL:			**POST CODE**	

If you would prefer to pay by credit card, please complete:
Please debit my Visa/Access/Diner's Card/American Express (delete as applicable) card no:

Signature ....

Expiry Date: ....

If you would NOT like to receive further information o̶̶ ̶ ̶ ̶ucts please tick the box. ❑

I LEFT MY SNEAKERS IN DIMENSION X

Bruce Coville

Rod Allbright's cousin Elspeth arrives for a visit the day after school finishes for the summer. Rod thinks his holidays will be ruined, but after they are kidnapped to Dimension X by a monster named Smorkus Flinders, Rod realizes that Elspeth is the least of his problems. After all, what's a bratty cousin compared to cranky monsters, furious aliens and the discovery that he is stuck in the middle of an interstellar power play?

And that doesn't begin to take into account the horrifying personal decision that Rod will be forced to make before his adventures are over . . .